She was pure torture

Derek was in trouble, his promise of temporary celibacy close to being forgotten. How was he going to turn away from Sydney tonight, when all he wanted to do was carry her off to bed?

Quickly he killed the engine and turned to face her. The look in her eyes held him spellbound.

Sex. Hot damp bodies, tangled sheets, anything-goes sex.

Immediately his body hardened and he ached with a powerful need to have her. She was making him forget his good intentions.

He exited the car and came round to help her from the vehicle. Her eyes held his as she slid from the seat.

Hot damp bodies, tangled sheets, anything-goes sex.

Sydney strode past him then glanced over her shoulder. "Coming?" she asked innocently. He groaned at the sinful note in her voice.

"Friends," he muttered as he bounded up the path toward her. "We're just supposed to be friends."

On the porch he stopped in front of her, trapping her within the heat of his body. Her lips parted and he clamped his mouth on hers in demanding possession. "Friends be damned...."

Hot damp bodies, tangled sheets, anything-goes sex.

Dear Reader,

Writing Sydney and Derek's romance was a lot of fun! I first got the story idea while waiting in an airport lounge. Two women were chatting about having kids, but without husbands to complicate the picture. Quickly I began jotting notes. What could be *more* fun than a sexy scientist with marriage on his mind *and* a feisty independent woman intent on having a baby but no hubby?

I hope you enjoy *The Seduction of Sydney*. I really love writing for Temptation because I can create a very sexy, upbeat contemporary story, especially in the BLAZE books.

In February 2000 look for my next release, #767 *Valentine Fantasy*, which is part of the FANTASY FOR HIRE miniseries kicking off in December 1999 with #759 *Christmas Fantasy* by Janelle Denison. Janelle and I had a great time creating the strapping sexy McBride brothers and their romantic fantasy business geared *just* for women!

Happy Reading!

Jamie Denton

P.S. I love to hear from my readers! Please write to me at P.O. Box 224, Mohall, ND 58761 or at jamiedenton@weluvromance.com

THE SEDUCTION OF SYDNEY
Jamie Denton

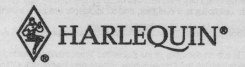

HARLEQUIN®

TORONTO • NEW YORK • LONDON
AMSTERDAM • PARIS • SYDNEY • HAMBURG
STOCKHOLM • ATHENS • TOKYO • MILAN • MADRID
PRAGUE • WARSAW • BUDAPEST • AUCKLAND

For AJ, Mike and Tim
With all my love,
Mom

ISBN 0-373-25848-8

THE SEDUCTION OF SYDNEY

Copyright © 1999 by Jamie Ann Denton.

This edition published by arrangement with Harlequin Books S.A.

® and TM are trademarks of the publisher. Trademarks indicated with
® are registered in the United States Patent and Trademark Office, the
Canadian Trade Marks Office and in other countries.

Visit us at www.romance.net

Printed in U.S.A.

THE WOMAN of his dreams was coated in mud. Derek bit the inside of his lip to keep from smiling. Even covered nearly head to toe in dried, caked-on mud, she was still the most exciting woman he knew.

And she had no clue how he felt about her.

"What happened this time?" he asked, opening the screen door. In the buttery glow of the porch light, he could see that her usually rich, silky sable hair was matted with mud. Portions of what had once been a teal silk dress peeked through the dirt and grime. Ripped black stockings covered most of her shapely legs. Mud-encrusted shoes dangled from the tips of her fingers.

He thought she was beautiful.

Sydney carefully stepped through the door and stopped at the edge of the ceramic tiled entryway. "You wouldn't believe it if I told you," she said, narrowing her bright green eyes.

He hid a smile. For the past few months, Sydney had been on an all-out search for a prince. To his delight, all she'd found so far was a procession of frogs. She was only twenty-eight. He didn't understand what the rush was all about. "Another tarnished knight in shining armor?" he asked, closing the door.

She rolled her eyes at his attempted humor.

"Can I take a shower?" She handed him her black pumps, one with a broken heel, then looked down at her ruined clothes and shook her head in disgust. "I need to clean up and have a cup of cocoa before I fill you in on the date from Hell."

He shouldn't be happy that her date had been another in a long line of disasters, but he couldn't help himself. Every potential relationship that failed, made him all the more confident he could convince Sydney they belonged together. Of course, making her realize they were made for each other wasn't going to be easy.

He led the way toward the back of the house and the bathroom. "You know where everything is, right?" She should. She spent as much time at his place as she did her own little cottage behind the veterinary clinic she'd bought upon her return to Seattle nearly a year ago.

"I need some clothes." She held out the sides of the slinky silk dress to emphasize her point.

"I've got some sweats you might be able to wear," he offered, then went to retrieve the change of clothes. He found a pair of drawstring sweats that might work, along with a University of Washington sweatshirt. She was such a tiny thing, she'd be dwarfed by his clothes, but she needed something to put on after her shower. He thought of offering her his favorite bathrobe, but he didn't think he could stand the torture of knowing she was naked beneath the thin blue terry cloth.

He returned a few minutes later. She stood in the center of the bathroom, looking small and wounded beneath the harsh glare of the overhead lighting. The urge to pull her into his arms and comfort her overwhelmed him. Who was he kidding? *She* overwhelmed him. And unless he did something about it soon, he could lose her forever. Not that he'd ever had her, but she just might find some guy she thought qualified as Mr. Right if he didn't make his feelings for her known.

"Here ya go," he said, setting the clothes on the wicker hamper, not wanting to think about life without Sydney Travers.

She smiled and his stomach bottomed out. Couldn't the fool woman see that she turned him inside out? "If you need anything else, let me know."

"Thank you, Derek."

He paused outside the bathroom door and looked at her. Gratitude filled her gaze. Dammit, he didn't want her gratitude. He wanted *her*.

He closed the door then headed into the kitchen to make the cocoa. As he filled the teakettle and set it on the stove, he discarded a half-dozen ideas on how to let her know of his feelings for her. The problem was simple. She didn't see him in that way. She loved him, he knew, but not romantically. They'd been friends for years, and not once during their youth had he ever had any romantic designs on the neighborhood tomboy. When he'd gone off to the Massachusetts Institute of Technology on a full academic scholarship, they'd only seen each other during vacations and holidays when he'd managed to make it home from school. Two years after he'd gone east, she'd moved to Texas to attend college, then followed up with veterinary school in Kentucky while he'd continued his education in astrophysics.

By the time he'd returned to Seattle for a position at the University of Washington teaching physics, astronomy and a few other general science courses while following his dreams in the astrophysics research lab, she'd taken a job as a large-animal vet in the horse-racing country of Kentucky. They'd only kept in contact with the occasional correspondence, holiday card or phone call. Since his mother had moved to Arizona with her new husband, he'd purchased his childhood home from her. He'd been content with his life. He'd dated a few women, though nobody special. He thought he'd fulfilled most of his goals, until Sydney returned to take over a small-and-large-animal clinic on the edge of the city, turning his world, and him, inside out.

He pulled a mug from the cabinet, then poured in the contents of a packet of instant cocoa. He still didn't know how it had happened. When she'd called late last spring to tell him she was moving back to Seattle, he'd been jazzed that his old buddy Sydney was coming home. When she'd pulled up in front of his house two weeks later, he'd been unprepared for his body's instant reaction to her.

He shoved a hand roughly through his hair. The only answer he could find was that his old buddy Sydney had been replaced by a beautiful, sexy woman with more charms and feminine secrets than he'd ever dreamed possible. Granted he hadn't seen her in years, but he could have sworn her green eyes hadn't had that hint of sensuality in them the last time they'd been together. Nor could he remember her having skin softer than satin or curves more deadly than an icy mountain road.

He crossed the kitchen to the table and slipped the stack of tests he'd been grading into his briefcase. The old pipes rattled, groaned, then quieted once Sydney adjusted the taps. Images of her standing beneath the hot spray seized his mind. He squeezed his eyes shut, but his internal vision only sharpened. He imagined the water sluicing over her body, winding its way down her gentle curves. Then his imagination kicked into high gear as he envisioned his hands following the same path.

He sucked in a sharp breath and let it out slowly. Why was he torturing himself like this? Cripes, he was worse than a pubescent teenager with nothing but sex on the brain.

He looked at the digital clock on the microwave. It was only a few minutes past nine and he suspected her dinner plans had been aborted. He opened a can of chicken noodle soup and heated it on the stove, then started making a couple of grilled-ham-and-cheese sandwiches.

"Something smells absolutely heavenly," Sydney said when she emerged from the bathroom. She no longer resembled the bedraggled, mud-covered creature with fire in her eyes who had shown up on his doorstep twenty minutes ago. Just as he'd suspected, she was practically swimming in the sweats he'd given her. She'd rolled up the bottoms of the legs so they hung loose around her slender ankles. Her feet were bare, her toenails painted a sexy shade of hot-pink. The sweat-shirt hung past her thighs, and even though she'd rolled up the sleeves, they still covered her wrists. She looked adorable.

"Sit down," he said, turning back to the stove and willing his body under control. "I figured you might be hungry."

She pulled out a chair and sat at the table. "You know me too well, Derek."

He wondered what she'd say if she knew how much more he wanted to know her. Intimately know her. Know her like no other man would ever know her again. He pushed those thoughts from his mind, gave the soup one last stir, then set the spoon in the empty can and turned to face her. She bent forward and unwrapped the towel, her hair falling in a cascade of damp sable waves, nearly touching the floor. She finger-combed the thick strands, then using her nails, rubbed at her scalp. "Lord, this feels good," she muttered. "I think I had enough mud in my hair for a couple of adobe bricks."

He imagined her hair spread across a stark white pillowcase. He imagined caressing the thick dark strands as they made love. He imagined her smooth-as-silk skin beneath his hands, her body beneath his. He imagined...

His control slipped, and his blood heated. He was a scientist for crying out loud. Scientists didn't have runaway imaginations...or did they? he wondered, watching as she straightened, toss-ing her long hair carelessly behind her shoulders. Her full breasts pressed against the soft fabric of the sweatshirt, and even under the bulk that hid her curves, he could see she wasn't wearing a thing. His mouth went as dry as dust.

She looked up at him curiously, her delicate eyebrows pulled together in a frown. "Derek? You okay?"

He managed to nod, because he couldn't find his voice. He wanted her, bad. Somehow, someway, he'd have to let her know how much she meant to him.

The teakettle began to whistle, drawing his attention. Turning back to the stove, he filled the mug with steaming water, then dropped in three marshmallows and added a splash of milk to cool it. He flipped the grilled-ham-and-cheese sandwiches, then slid them onto a plate and sliced them in half with the edge of the spatula. After pouring the warmed soup into a bowl, he carried the impromptu meal to the table and set it in front of her. He'd never really mastered the art of cooking; his skills were generally limited to the bare necessities as a matter of survival. If it didn't come out of a can he could heat, a cardboard box he could microwave, or a container he could pick up on his way home from the university, he was lost in the kitchen, except for barbecued steak and grilled ham and cheese, his only culinary talents.

She closed her eyes and pulled in a breath. "You're too good to me."

She didn't know the half of it, he thought. He'd do anything in the world for her, if she'd let him.

"Tell me what happened." Hearing about her dates was a combination of relief and torture, but he just had to know.

"It was awful from the minute he picked me

up," she said, then bit into the grilled-cheese sandwich.

Her answer gave him comfort. "Who was it this time?"

"The Surgeon," she said, then polished off half of the sandwich.

She had an amusing habit of naming each of her dates according to their occupations. In the past three months, he'd heard tales of The Accountant, The Technical Writer, The Advertising Man, The X-Ray Tech and The Pediatrician. The Pediatrician had been promising and had lasted longer than the rest, all the way to Date Four. Most of her potential partners were lucky if they made it to Date Two before she found some major flaw in their character. The Pediatrician's potential had flown out the window when she'd learned he might enjoy providing medical treatment for children, but the best part of his job was sending the "screaming brats" home with their neurotic mothers.

"You're trying too hard," he told her. "I bet Mr. Right is right in front of you and you just haven't seen him yet."

She dipped her spoon into the chicken noodle soup. "I sure wish he'd show his face. I can't take much more of this. I'm convinced there just aren't any prime candidates out there."

"You make it sound like they're applying for a job."

She shrugged, then lowered her gaze and concentrated on finishing the soup, but not before he noted a spark of determination in her eyes. What could have her so determined to find Mr. Right?

He stood and went to the pantry, found her favorite brand of chocolate mini-doughnuts, which he kept on hand, then returned to the table. "What went wrong with The Surgeon?" he asked, sliding them in front of her.

Grinning her thanks, she tore open the package. She bit into the doughnut, closed her eyes and moaned her delight.

His libido skyrocketed again.

"The Surgeon," she said, dusting crumbs from the front of the sweatshirt, "is a jerk. You know, he doesn't even know how to change a tire? Completely helpless. A disgrace to his gender."

He chuckled, because he suspected she expected him to, but he didn't understand what the problem was with not being able to change a tire. Wasn't that why there were mechanics and tow truck drivers, to handle those sorts of problems?

She took another doughnut from the bag and ripped it in half. "He picks me up and he's early. Of course, I'm running behind. There was an emergency at the clinic this afternoon. Anyway, he made a reservation at La Petite near the Sound, and you know how difficult it is to get in there. If you're late, that cranky maître d' will give your table away. So, on the way there, all The Surgeon did was complain that we were going to lose our reservation. Then when we get a flat tire, he's acting like it's all my fault or something."

She popped half the doughnut into her mouth, then hesitated a moment before she shrugged and finished the second half while reaching for another.

"Sounds like a creep," he said, hoping he portrayed enough sympathy to hide the fact that he wanted to shout with glee.

"He is," she said, setting the doughnut on the plate in front of her. She reached for the mug of cocoa and peered at him over the rim. "I hit him with the crowbar."

Derek stared at her, dumbfounded. Sydney didn't have a mean bone in her body. Spirited, yes. Determined, most definitely. But violent? Never. Well, almost never, he amended, recalling the time she saw a street punk mistreating a stray dog. "You did what?" he asked carefully.

She grinned, her green eyes sparkling with mischief. "I hit him with the crowbar. It really was an accident," she added, lowering her mug. "Oh, but that's not the half of it. Like I said, this guy doesn't have a clue how to change a tire. And he didn't think to recharge the batteries in his cell phone. That is unheard of for someone in his position. So we're standing on the shoulder of the freeway, and when I tell him that I've changed tires before and could show him how, he still says that he can't do it."

She shifted in the chair, then pulled her legs up to her chest and wrapped her arms around her knees. "He's a surgeon," she said in mock severity. "So I remind him that I perform surgeries every day, too, and you know what the creep says?"

He leaned back in the chair and crossed his arms over his chest. "I can imagine," he muttered.

"He says that my hands are hardly as valuable as his. Like what I do is incomparable to the saving of human life. As if animals have no value," she complained, her voice rising slightly in outrage and disbelief.

Derek smiled. Oh, yeah. The Surgeon was definitely out of the running. "Told you he was a creep. Is that when you hit him with the crowbar?"

She shook her head. "Not yet. But, by this time I do have the crowbar in my hand and I'm seriously thinking of bonking him one on the head."

"So when *did* you hit him?"

She shifted again and reached for her cocoa. "I'm getting to that," she said, sitting crosslegged in the chair. "I got the tire off, and he just stands there with his hands on his hips and has the nerve to complain that if I hadn't been late in the first place, even though we'd gotten a flat tire, we still would have made it to the restaurant in time for our reservation."

"So then you hit him with the crowbar?"

"I should have, but no. I asked him to get the spare for me, and he refused."

"His hands again?"

Sydney nodded. "Uh-huh. Said he could injure them."

"Then you hit him."

She smiled and he knew he'd never tire of her beautiful, wicked grin. "Not yet. I didn't say anything, but I'm thinking to myself that this guy is the most arrogant creep I've ever had the misfortune of meeting. I go to the trunk and manage to get the spare out, but I rip my nylons and get this horrible black skid mark on my dress. I lean the tire against the rear panel of the car, and the creep makes some snide comment about how he supposes we'll have to go back to my house so I can change into something more respectable."

"Then you hit him."

"Not yet," she said, still grinning. She slipped a strand of hair behind her ear and leaned forward, her face animated as she continued to regale him with the details of her disastrous evening.

"I told him I thought it'd be best if he just took me home—period. Did he really think that I was going to spend an evening with him after this? Then the arrogant jerk actually has the gall to suggest that we go back to my place and...and have sex! *That's* when I hit him."

Derek frowned. "In the head, I hope."

"No. On the foot. I was so stunned by his lewd suggestion, I dropped the crowbar on his foot."

"That's not so bad." He wished she had hit him upside the head, he thought jealously.

Sydney bit her lip, trying to be serious. "The forked end," she said, a smile flirting around the corners of her mouth.

Derek winced. "That's bad."

She giggled. "I think I broke his toe."

He wanted to break the guy's neck, but kept the thought to himself. "That still doesn't explain how you got all muddy."

She finished off the cocoa then reached for another chocolate doughnut. "I took off while he was dancing around holding his foot in his *precious* surgeon hands. I made it to the end of the closest off-ramp when a big rig came around the corner. Just my luck, there was a huge puddle."

"Why didn't you find a phone and call me? You know I would've picked you up."

She stood and cleared the dishes, setting them in the sink. "I was too angry to think straight. Besides, it wasn't that far."

"Not far?" He shot from the chair and faced her. "I'm about four miles from the freeway. That's a hell of a walk, not to mention it's not safe to be out at night by yourself."

She crossed her arms over her chest and lifted her chin defiantly. "I can take care of myself."

He blew out a frustrated stream of breath. Sydney was as free-spirited as they came, and there was no such thing as taming her. That was the problem with The Accountant, The Surgeon and all the others she'd taken on test drives. They wanted to control her, to tame her spirit.

Fools, he thought.

He didn't want to control her. All he wanted to do was love her.

"Come on," he said, snagging his keys from the hook by the kitchen door. "I'll give you a ride home."

He opened the door and waited for her to precede him. Bronson, his nine-month-old Doberman pinscher pup, lumbered down from his favorite napping spot on the back porch, which just happened to be Derek's favorite lawn chair. The dog trotted across the concrete patio, his stubby tail wagging enthusiastically at the sight of his favorite veterinarian.

"Hey there, Bronson," Sydney greeted the dog. She crouched low and waited for Bronson to come to her.

Derek had found the dog, abandoned and sickly outside the university lab about six months ago. Thanks to Sydney's diligence, the pup had been nursed back to health. He'd never planned on owning a dog, but when Sydney had told him *his* dog was ready to come home, he hadn't quibbled. Now he owned a dog.

"Is Derek taking good care of you?" she crooned to Bronson, rubbing her hands over his thick back.

Bronson sat and looked at Derek with big brown eyes.

"Oh, all right." Once Bronson heard the jangle of keys he'd never be able to leave without him, anyway. "But you're sitting in the back seat this time," he warned.

As if he understood every word, Bronson shot across the patio to Derek's Explorer.

"I guess that answers my question," Sydney said with a laugh and stood. "You definitely have spoiled him rotten."

Derek grinned. Did she know how gorgeous she was when she smiled? Did she know that she drove him crazy with wanting her? "Yeah, just call me Professor Marshmallow."

She closed the space separating them and laid her hand over his arm. His pulse rate kicked into high gear at her gentle touch. "You're not a marshmallow, Derek. You're a good-hearted person, and I love you. You're my best friend."

He placed his hand over hers and looked down into her bright emerald gaze. "I love you, too, Syd," he said, but he didn't mean platonic love. He loved her, *really* loved her.

Her smile wavered and she looked away.

"We'd better get going," he said, hoping he hadn't made her feel awkward. Had she guessed his true feelings? Had he been that transparent? As much as he wanted her to know how he really felt about her, he couldn't help be worried that if she knew, it could cause irreparable harm to their long-standing friendship.

That was a risk he was going to have to take...as soon as he figured out how to make her realize she couldn't live without him.

SYDNEY HATED blind dates. The only thing worse than a blind date was the fact that she was beginning to feel just desperate enough to agree to one. When her assistant, Rachel, suggested she might have something in common with her husband's brother's wife's cousin, she'd reluctantly agreed. After all, The Lawyer couldn't be any worse than The Surgeon she'd left on the shoulder of the freeway a week ago.

She added a few last strokes of mascara to her lashes, wondering why she was putting herself through this much misery. When she had made the decision to have a baby, she'd had no idea of the difficulty she'd face in finding an intelligent man willing to father a child with no strings attached. She had been so sure there'd be no shortage of willing participants once she found someone she deemed appropriate breeding stock. The last thing she'd planned on had been the development of a conscience by the males of the species. Things had certainly changed since high school.

So far in her quest she'd found only two potential paternal consorts remotely close to serious consideration. The Pediatrician had been the front-runner, until she'd gotten up the nerve to tell him that she wanted a baby. He was just arrogant enough that she thought he'd be more than willing to cooperate by fathering a child with no strings attached. Then he'd told her he really didn't like children all that much and had taken steps to ensure he'd never have any of his own. Not only had she been appalled by his declaration considering his profession, she'd been just a tad disappointed. The actual breeding process would no doubt have been quite enjoyable.

She sighed, then applied a light dusting of blush to her cheekbones. Dark hair and blue eyes combined with a well-toned body and a heap of intelligence didn't carry much weight if there was nothing substantial behind it. Looks weren't everything, she told herself firmly, applying a light coat of mauve lipstick to her lips. The father of her baby needed to be compassionate and caring, as well as intelligent.

The Accountant had been another prospect, and she'd even broached the subject on their second date. He'd droned on and on about the costs involved in raising a child, told her which investments would gain her the most bang for her buck toward a college fund, but in the end, he'd declined her "very generous offer" on a matter of principle.

There had to be a man out there somewhere willing to father a child, she thought as she slipped on a thin pair of gold hoop earrings. It wasn't as if she were asking for a lifelong commitment. A set of matching bands was the last thing on her mind. She'd been that route, or what she'd believed had been very close to it, once. A walk down the aisle was not on her list of wants or needs. All she wanted was a baby. No strings, no demands, just a baby.

"What you need is a sperm donor," she quipped to her reflection, then fluffed her bangs.

Her hands stilled. A sperm donor, she thought. Slowly, she lowered her hands and braced them on the marble counter. Leaning forward, she stared at her reflection. Why hadn't she thought of that before? It wasn't as if she were unattractive and couldn't find a man. She just didn't want, or need, a man in her life. Nor could she find one unprincipled enough to accommodate her.

Well, she amended, there *were* plenty of unprincipled men out there, she just didn't want any of *them* fathering her child.

The doorbell chimed. She'd have to give this donor idea more thought. But for now, she had a blind date with The Lawyer. She rolled her eyes heavenward, wondering if there was a patron saint to oversee blind dates.

She left the bathroom and grabbed her purse from the dresser on her way out of the bedroom. The heels of her new black pumps clicked on the hardwood floor as she hurried down the hallway to the front door. Her hand reached for the doorknob and she pasted what she hoped was a smile on her face.

God, she hated blind dates.

She opened the door and prayed her smile

didn't falter as she tipped her head back and looked up at the towering height of The Lawyer. She had to take a step back to really get a good look at him, since he stood at least a foot and a half taller than her five foot three.

"Why, you must be Mz. Sydney," he drawled, in the heaviest Southern accent she'd ever encountered despite her years in Kentucky. "Rachel said you were a perty little thang. She sure wasn't lyin'."

Sydney was positive her grin turned to a grimace when he raked his pecan-colored eyes down the length of her body. "Would you like to come in?" she asked, hoping he didn't smack his balder than a cue ball head on her door frame. "Hubert."

"That's mighty friendly of ya, Mz. Sydney," Hubert Longfellow said in what she determined was more than a drawl, it was a nasally drawl. "But the barbecue's gonna be cold if we don't hurry-ep."

"Barbecue?" she questioned, then took a good look at what the Jolly Green Giant meets Mr. Clean was wearing. A red-plaid shirt spanned his narrow chest and was tucked neatly into a pair of crisp jeans that were just short enough that she could make out the pattern of argyle socks. Rachel had told her Hubert was taking her to dinner. She'd assumed that meant a restaurant and had dressed appropriately. From the look of Hubert, she was overdressed in her slim black skirt and red silk blouse.

"There's a Western grill about five miles from the city," Hubert explained. "Best dang barbecued ribs in the state." He frowned, his thin brows colliding. "You ain't one of them there tofu and sprout eatin' types, are ya now, Mz. Sydney? I like a woman with an appetite. A real appetite."

Save me from matchmaking assistants, she thought, then managed a grin. "No, I'm not a vegetarian. Barbecue will be fine."

As she stepped onto the covered porch and turned to lock the front door, she had a feeling it was going to be a very long evening, indeed.

2

"HE DID WHAT?"

"Stop laughing," Sydney ordered Derek as she poured him another cup of coffee. "It wasn't funny. He could have been hurt."

She scowled at her closest friend as he fought, and failed, to hide the grin tugging at his lips. She slipped the carafe back onto the warming plate of the coffeemaker, then sat across from him at the kitchen table. She couldn't recall exactly when the tradition had first begun, but Sunday mornings were reserved for breakfast with Derek. Like clockwork, each Sunday he'd arrive with fresh-baked muffins, the Sunday paper and Bronson.

She snagged a raspberry muffin from the pink bakery box and sliced it in half. "The Lawyer wasn't all that bad," she muttered, slipping Bronson a small piece of muffin. "Just a little... clumsy."

Derek's bark of laughter caused her frown to deepen and Bronson to prick his ears forward. "If you're not more discriminating in your choice of dates, Syd," Derek teased, "you're going to have to replace your entire wardrobe. This makes what? Three outfits ruined by would-be knights in shining armor this month alone?"

"Would you please stop it," she ordered again, but the laughter in her voice contradicted her words. "He didn't mean to dump his plate on me. And he really could have been hurt when he tripped."

Derek's laughter deepened, the sound rumbling along her nerve endings in a way that was far from unpleasant. She wrote off the sensation to her melancholy mood.

His sapphire eyes filled with laughter. "I bet he didn't mean to smear butter all over your blouse, either," he gasped once he stopped laughing. He was enjoying her disastrous date just a little too much.

Sydney set her muffin aside and sighed, propping her chin in her hand. "You know, I think I've about given up on finding the right person."

Derek sobered. He reached across the table and laid his hand over hers. She looked down at his long, tapered fingers as they gently squeezed her hand. An achy emptiness filled her, but she figured it was caused by the strong desire to have a child and finding no potential paternity candidates within a fifty-mile radius.

"Syd, what's the big rush?"

She twisted her hand in his and laced their fingers together. A series of little tingles danced up her arm when she pressed their palms together. "My biological clock is ticking."

He gave her a sidelong look and his mouth quirked into an amused half smile. "At twenty-eight?"

She pulled her hand from his, telling herself those dancing tingles and the small flashes of heat that shot through her meant nothing. "You wouldn't understand," she said, hating the wistful catch to her voice.

She thought about telling him the truth behind the series of disappointing dates she'd had in the past few months, for all of two seconds. Derek might be her closest friend, but he was a man first, and she hardly expected him to understand what she was feeling. He didn't know about Nicholas and how she'd fallen victim to his charm and his lies. He didn't know that she'd been played the fool in the worst possible way. Nor did she expect him to understand that she'd hardly slept last night because she'd been weighing the pros and cons of artificial insemination.

Compassion lit his sapphire gaze and her heart twisted just a little. "Try me," he prompted, his voice as soft as velvet.

She blew out a stream of breath that caused her bangs to flutter against her forehead. The smile she gave him was wry at best. "I guess it's a woman thing," she said, and stood to clear away their breakfast dishes.

She set the dishes in the sink and looked through the open kitchen window to the small yard beyond. A rainbow of tulips bloomed along the wooden fence at the rear of the yard; she'd planted the bulbs last fall. The roses she'd put in when she'd first moved into the cottage nearly a year ago were just beginning to bud with the promise of new life. Black-eyed Susans and a profusion of pansies grew along both sides of the narrow cobblestone pathway that led to a small concrete patio behind the single-car garage. She treasured her little house as much as she did her veterinary clinic. The only missing component of her life was a child.

She wasn't certain she'd like the dispassionate atmosphere of a sperm clinic in choosing an appropriate donor for her future child, but time was running out. As she'd told Derek, her biological clock was ticking, and becoming louder by the day. The alarm might not be set to sound off, but she wanted to have a child before she turned thirty. Her parents had had her late in life, and she knew what it was like to have a mother who thought she was too old to participate in all the mother-daughter activities that arose during youth. She knew how hard it had been on her parents raising a teenager in their fifties and into their early sixties. Plus, she didn't want to have to worry about age being a health concern during pregnancy, as it had been for her mother. She was young, healthy and financially secure. The time was right, even if there was no potential daddy material in sight. Perhaps the idea of artificial insemination wasn't half as crazy as she'd first thought.

"...this week."

She turned and looked at Derek. He stood with his back to her, the coffee mug clutched in his hand as he scanned the newspaper. Faded denim clung to the cutest behind she'd seen in weeks. *When did he get such an adorable tush?* she wondered, and frowned.

He turned and stared at her. "Syd, you okay?"

Her frown deepened and she looked at him. *Such a nice mouth*, she thought, and wondered what it'd be like to be kissed by Derek. Not one of those friendly kisses he always gave her in greeting, but a real tongue-tangling kiss filled with wicked promise.

"Syd?"

"Did you say something?" she asked.

He grinned, and she crossed her arms and leaned against the counter. He really was good-looking. She supposed he always had been gorgeous, but he was her best friend. She just never thought of him as hunk material. He was sweet, smart and darn it, he was sexy, too. Why hadn't she noticed that until now?

"Do you want to catch a movie this week?" he asked, turning back to the table to scan the movie section of the newspaper.

A shock of black hair fell across his forehead as he bent over the paper. He muttered something about an action flick, but she was too busy noticing the way the back of his hair teased his collar to pay much attention. Heck, now that she thought about it, she'd never noticed the width of his shoulders, either, or how wide his chest was, or how it tapered down to trim hips and that cute behind.

Good grief, what was wrong with her? She really was getting desperate!

"Whatever you want is fine with me," she muttered, focusing on the way the muscles in his back bunched against the cotton fabric of his huntergreen T-shirt when he straightened and drained the last of his coffee.

She watched, mesmerized, as he reached for the coffeepot and refilled his mug, unable to shake the thought that he could be the solution to her problem....

Derek fathering her child had merit, but she quickly discarded the notion as ridiculous. Derek Buchanan, Ph.D., was her best friend, and the last thing she wanted to do was ruin their friendship by asking him to make love to her.

No. Not make love. Father a child. Yes, that's what she wanted. Someone to father a child.

She frowned again. The idea of making love to Derek suddenly held a great deal of appeal.

She shook the silly thought from her mind. This baby business was definitely getting to her. There was no other logical explanation for her wild lapse of common sense.

She hoped.

"THESE BINDERS contain the biographical details of our donors." The sperm bank counselor set a thick three-ring binder on the oak desk in front of Sydney. "We encourage you to choose several you find appropriate, then narrow your search from there."

Sydney flipped open the binder and glanced down at the computer printout that contained the standard information on weight and height along with hair and eye color. The list also contained hobbies and interests, likes and dislikes, allergies, aspirations and even the family medical history and general background information of each potential donor. "Can I take them home?" she asked.

The counselor's wire-framed bifocals went down and her thick gray brows shot upward.

Heat burned Sydney's cheeks. "Copies." She tapped her finger frantically on the donor bio. "Can I take home *copies* of the ones that appeal...I mean the ones I think have potential?" Her blush deepened. She was a doctor, for crying out loud. A veterinarian, but still a doctor who dealt with biology on a daily basis. Blushing should have been beyond her.

Obviously it wasn't.

The counselor smiled. "I'm sorry, Ms. Travers, but our files are confidential. If there's nothing here that appeals to you, we suggest you come again to review our donors. We receive several new donations each week."

Sydney didn't want to think about what *that* statement meant, but couldn't help herself. She imagined a sterile room with a VCR and a selection of movies with titles like *Space Sluts from Venus* or *Bimbos Are Us*. Plastic cups placed in paper bags in exchange for cash on the barrel. She gave the counselor a weak smile and tried not to imagine an array of gentlemen's magazines meant to stimulate while the donors took matters into their own hands.

"If you have no further questions, I'll leave you alone to look over the donors we have available. I'll check back with you shortly."

Sydney nodded, then waited until she was alone before perusing the statistical information in front of her. After giving the idea a lot of thought, she had decided artificial insemination was the best choice for her and not a last resort or an act of desperation. She thought of it as making a choice, a choice to have a child. On her own, without a husband, or having to share the raising of her child with an occasional or weekend father. If there was one thing she knew deep in her bones it was that marriage was definitely not an option.

When she'd visited her gynecologist the previous morning and explained what she wanted, he'd spoken to her at length about her decision. Once he'd been convinced of her sincerity, he'd given her the name of the clinic. If she found a suitable donor, they could perform the insemination this coming Friday.

She flipped the pages in the binder and read the information on each of the sperm donors. Thirty minutes later, she'd narrowed her search down to an even dozen.

She inspected the bios she'd selected, then discarded another five. While looks weren't that important to her, she tended to go for blue eyes and dark hair, a trait common to the last seven spread on the desk in front of her.

She viewed the family histories, then slipped numbers two, five and six back into the binder. Number one's father was prematurely bald, so she set him aside, as well. If she had a son, the least she could do was guarantee him hair past thirty-five.

She made a face and returned number four to the binder. Under the heading Special Interests he listed himself as a card-carrying member of a radical racist group. Goodness, how had she missed that horror the first time around?

The door opened and the counselor stepped back inside the office. "Are you finding our donors to your liking, Ms. Travers?"

Sydney took a deep breath and examined the remaining two in front of her. Number seven was an offensive lineman at the University of Washington. He weighed in at a mere 246 pounds. Good heavens, she'd give birth to a buffalo. And if she had a girl… She shook her head and set number seven aside.

Number three was a grad student in the field of journalism and communications. He listed television broadcasting as his career choice. Obviously a looker, she thought, and scanned his physical description. An ambitious man, too, goal-oriented like herself. She viewed his family history again and saw nothing to send up a red flag.

She stood and handed the last bio to the counselor. This time, her smile was heartfelt.

"I'll take him."

SYDNEY HUGGED her knees to her chest and fought another rush of tears. She'd managed to hold them at bay ever since she'd left her gynecologist's office following the insemination procedure, but now she gave in and allowed the hot tears their freedom.

She had no business crying; the decision she'd made wasn't one she'd ever regret, nor had it been made lightly. She'd chosen to have a child. After the series of disappointing dates and a fruitless search, selecting an anonymous donor had been the best possible solution, and thanks to medical science, in a matter of days she'd know whether or not she had conceived.

If she had everything she'd ever wanted, then why did she feel so darned miserable?

She wiped at the tears with the back of her hand. Hormonal imbalance, she told herself. She always got a little weepy during the ovulation stage of her cycle, but she suspected the reason went far deeper than an overabundance of estrogen.

Monday, when she'd made the appointment with her gynecologist, her timing couldn't have been more perfect. She'd be ovulating in three days. Tuesday she'd selected the donor, and on Thursday she'd had the appropriate tests to determine she was indeed ovulating.

With nothing but green lights ahead, bright and early this morning she'd arrived at Stewart Hutchinson's office for the procedure that would forever change her life. During the past twenty-four hours, she'd run the gamut of emotions, from excited to nervous to terrified that she was making a mistake, then she'd start the emotional cycle all over again. By the time she'd shaken the doubts and convinced herself that every woman in her position would feel the same, she'd been wearing an air-conditioned gown and had a sterile blue cloth draped over her abdomen and legs, awaiting Stewart's arrival with the daddy-to-go.

She had gone through with her plan, but she felt wretched. She didn't regret her decision. Nothing could make her change her mind about having a baby. But she was alone. Utterly and completely alone, and it hadn't hit her until she was changing back into her own clothes following the procedure. She'd lost her parents two years ago, her mother first, then her father six months later. She'd been an only child and had no relatives, other than one childless and widowed aunt whom she hadn't seen since she was sixteen when they'd gone on a family vacation to Florida. Her child would have no one, except her. No grandparents, no uncles or aunts or cousins. And unless she decided to repeat the insemination process in a few years, the chances of a sibling were slim to none.

She and her child would be alone, except of course, for Derek. For as long as she could remember, Derek had always been a part of her life. She couldn't recall what age she'd been when he'd moved into the old Elmer Piedmont place with his mother, but ever since that first day when the moving van had pulled up across the street from her parents' house, she and Derek had been friends, and had remained so for twenty years or more.

The thought of Derek sobered her, and she peered into the dusky darkness of the living room to the clock above the television set. He'd be picking her up for the movies in about half an hour. The doctor had told her she needn't curb her activities, just refrain from anything too strenuous for a few days. Sitting in a darkened movie theater hardly qualified as strenuous.

Wiping the last of the tears from her face, she decided she was just feeling a little sorry for herself. She wouldn't be alone, and neither would her child. They'd always have Derek.

She flipped on a lamp so he'd know she was home, then headed into the bathroom to wash her face and touch up her makeup before he arrived. As she filled the basin with cool water, she wondered what he'd say when she told him she'd been artificially inseminated. He'd support her decision, or at least she expected him to be supportive.

If Derek was anything, he was nonjudgmental.

DEREK PULLED HIS Explorer into an empty parking spot a block and a half from the theater. A light rain fell, typical for Seattle in June, but even the rain couldn't dampen his spirit, because tonight was the night.

No more procrastinating, no more avoidance tactics. Tonight, he'd lay his heart on the line. Tonight, he'd let her know they were made for each other and it was high time she realized it.

He'd been unable to think of anything else all day. He'd recalculated the formulas on the absolute magnitudes study his lab was conducting at least a half dozen times, but the only fundamental measurements he'd been concerned with were those of one very sexy veterinarian. He'd even tried to perfect his speech for the lecture he was slated to give at the University of California at Berkeley during the astrophysicist conference the following week. Preparation for the symposium on the basic properties of measuring the strength and velocity of atmospheric optical turbulence had been nothing more than an exercise in futility.

For so long he'd thought the only problem he had with Sydney was determining the right approach to take. During the past few months, he'd attempted to show her how he felt about her in a variety of ways, hoping to penetrate that wall she'd erected around herself since her return to Seattle. Subtleties hadn't worked. The only option left was the direct approach. Following the movie they'd have a late supper, and then he'd tell her.

He shut off the engine and turned to face her. She stared out the window, a dreamy expression on her beautiful face. Her hair was held back with a gold clip in an attempt to tame her long sable curls. He itched to take that clip and toss it aside so he could bury his hands in the silken length of her hair and let it sift through his fingers.

She sighed, then turned to look at him, the dreamy expression segueing into an even dreamier smile. The light scent of her perfume teased him, lured him, and he resisted the urge to dip his head and taste her deeply, seeing for himself if she was as sweet as he'd imagined.

He shoved the fantasy to the back of his mind and opened the driver's side door, taking in a deep breath of cool, rain-freshened air, hoping to cool his libido, as well. He circled the truck to open her door, but she'd already beat him to it and stood waiting for him on the wet pavement.

Her smile faded and a frown creased her brow. "Did you hear that?" she asked.

He listened, but heard nothing except the noise of city traffic. "Hear what?"

"That," she said, straining for some sound that was beyond his range of hearing.

"I don't hear anything," he said, and pocketed his keys.

She turned and hurried down the sidewalk toward an alley, stopping at the opening between two brick buildings. Before he could guess her intent, she slipped into the darkness and disappeared.

He jogged after her, prepared to upbraid her about the dangers of entering a dark alley at night, until he found her crouched beside a trash bin. He crept up behind her and looked over her shoulder to a litter of newly born pups. Now that he was close, he heard their weak mewling. How she'd heard them from the busy street was a mystery to him.

"Give me your jacket." She didn't look at him but held her hand out for the jacket. "We have to take them back to the clinic. They'll never make it through the night if we leave them here."

Knowing it'd do no good to argue with her, he slipped out of his jacket and handed it to her, stilling when he heard a deep, threatening growl.

"Uh-oh," he said, looking over his shoulder to see a large, shaggy dog with teeth bared. "Looks like mama's home."

She reached up and laid her hand over his arm. "Put these puppies on your jacket," she instructed, her voice low and calm. Slowly, so as not to alarm the growling mother dog, she stood and stepped around him.

Sydney was a vet for one reason only, her deep love of animals. He'd seen her face down an angry animal before, and he shouldn't be surprised that she planned to do just that now. But they were messing with this dog's babies, and if there was one thing he'd learned from hanging out with Sydney for the past twenty-two years, you don't mess with a mama or her babies, of any species.

"What do you think you're doing?" he asked in a harsh whisper.

"She's hurt," she said, not taking her eyes off the wounded dam. "There's too much blood."

"She just gave birth. Of course there's—"

"No," she said, inching closer to the dog and ignoring the guttural growls. "She's injured. Look at her hind quarter."

He did, and saw the odd twist to the dog's back leg. The dog hobbled backward, her growls deepening as she showed more of her teeth. She was not only hurt and afraid, but protective of her brood. This was not a good situation, but he didn't know how to divert Sydney to keep her away from danger. When it came to animals, the woman had no fear.

"You're going to get bitten," he warned.

She gave him a look that said what she thought of that statement, then continued her slow approach toward the dam, speaking in soft, soothing tones. The dog would have none of it, her growl deepening until she finally issued a rough snarl and lunged toward Sydney.

Derek's stomach bottomed out and he reached for Sydney, hauling her away from the dog. Pulling his keys from his pocket, he slapped them in her palm.

"Get the puppies into the truck," he ordered, his heart beating like a drum. Before he had time to think about what he was doing, he stalked across the alley to the dam. She growled, but tucked her tail between her legs. He noted a small, timid movement of her tail that could be construed as a wag, then he lifted the dog in his arms, careful not to further injure her leg.

"Let's go," he said. Sydney quickly gathered the pups in her arms, then followed him out of the alley to the truck.

3

SYDNEY PULLED off the surgical gloves and tossed them into the waste bin. The dam had obviously been hit by a car. Her back leg had been fractured in two places, but that hadn't been the more serious problem. The leg would have healed, but the internal injuries, combined with what Sydney determined had been premature labor and delivery caused by the trauma of the accident, had taken its toll on the large, scruffy dog. She'd used all her skills to try to save the mother, but in the end, the dam just hadn't been strong enough to survive the numerous injuries.

She disconnected the trunk and removed the IVs, then looked over the operating table to Derek. His eyes filled with compassion. "There's nothing else you could've done for her," he said quietly.

Despite her efforts not to cry, a tear escaped and wound it's way down her cheek. He circled the table and pulled her into his arms. She went willingly, slipping her arms around his middle, greedily accepting the comfort he offered.

"You did your best," he said, then pressed his lips against her temple. His hands slid up and down her back in a soothing, reassuring motion until finally, the tension of the past twenty-four hours began to ebb.

Resting her cheek against his wide chest, she heard the steady rhythm of his heart. The horrible pain in her chest went deeper than losing a patient. She thought about the seven orphaned puppies in the warmer across the hall from the surgery, and how they'd just lost their mother. They were alone. Just as her baby would be alone if anything happened to her. She knew she was being ridiculous, but the loss of the dam reminded her of how fragile life could be, how in a matter of seconds it could all end.

She pulled back and looked into Derek's handsome face. He was so strong. She saw it in the squareness of his jaw, in the nose that was just a tad crooked because an explosion in the high school chemistry lab had thrown him halfway across the room. He was strong. Rock steady. And Lord, she needed his strength right now, but more importantly, she needed the reassurance that he'd always be there for her, no matter what.

He moved his hands from her back to cup her face. The touch of his palms against her skin was warm, but the look in his eyes went beyond warm. It was hot, she thought as the pads of his thumbs brushed the tears from her cheeks.

Before she could guess his intent, he dipped his head and pressed his lips against hers. This wasn't like his typical kiss of greeting. This was a kiss meant to entice, to incite heat and make a woman forget everything but the man holding her in his arms.

And forget she did.

Maybe it was the strong sense of loneliness that had plagued her for the better part of the day, that caused her to wreathe her arms around his neck and press her body against the solidness of his. Or maybe it was something as simple as passion lain dormant being sparked to life and making her common sense flee. That was the only explanation she could summon when he slipped his tongue between her lips and she didn't even think of stopping him. Instead, she kissed him back with a hunger that should have taken her by surprise, but felt all too natural and welcome. She reveled in the hunger, in the need and the feel of his firm wide chest pressed against her aching and heavy breasts.

She clung to him when he lifted her in his arms to carry her out of the surgery and down the hall to her office. She nuzzled his neck and pressed light teasing kisses along the thick, corded column of his throat. She needed him, wanted him with a ferocity that reached inside to places she'd forgotten existed. He touched her, the core of her, the very center of her, where her heart had resided in quiet loneliness far too long.

"Don't," she whispered when he reached out to turn on the light. She traced the shell of his ear with the tip of her tongue. He groaned, a low, deep growl that told her he was as affected as she by their foreplay.

Carefully, as if she were the most fragile of china, he laid her on the sofa in her office and followed her down onto the soft, worn leather. A stream of fluorescent light intruded into the room from the corridor, and she could see the hunger and passion blazing in his eyes. A hunger and passion that equaled the currents raging through her.

The need to be close, to feel that ultimate connection with another human being drove her. She needed to feel that connection with Derek in the most elemental way. Then, just maybe, she wouldn't feel so alone.

His arms were braced on either side of her, his hands gently smoothing her hair from her face. She loved his touch, reveled in it and the tenderness commingling with the heat of his gaze. She loved the way he made her feel, the delicious pressure that tightened her belly and made her feel alive in his arms.

"This will change everything." The warm, husky undertone of his voice skirted along her nerve endings.

She tugged on his shirt until her hands pressed against the tightened muscles of his back. "I know," she whispered, her voice breaking with emotion. "I want you to make love to me, Derek."

Her heart gave a distinct thump at the very male look that flashed in his eyes. The awareness between them was as unexpected as a summer snowstorm, but a million times more welcome. She didn't think to question what was happening between them; every coherent thought escaped her when he traced the outline of her lips with his tongue. Gradually, he deepened the sensual caress until swift, penetrating strokes filled her, causing the pressure inside her to build into an insistent ache of need. A need only he had the power to satisfy.

The warmth of his big body surrounded her as

he held her, caressed her and drove her wild with desire. Soon kisses and caresses were no longer enough. They undressed each other quickly, as if any parting of their bodies was too long to be separated. When they came together, it was in an explosion of heat and fierce desire. He settled between her thighs, the hard length of him pressing intimately against her. She wove one hand into his thick black hair, and pulled him down for a hot, openmouthed kiss while she reached for him. He moaned deep in his throat when she held him, hot, hard and throbbing.

Derek thought he was going to explode if he didn't have her soon. He hadn't meant to kiss her back in the surgery, but the lost look in her tear-brightened gaze had tugged at his heart until his only thought had been to offer her comfort in the only way he knew how. The physical contact had been his undoing. Her scent had wrapped around him, sending his equilibrium and common sense into a tailspin. What had begun as a slow swell of desire, erupted until sharp and insistent need clawed at his gut.

"Now, Derek," she demanded in a throaty whisper that nearly sent him careening over the edge.

With his mouth pressed against hers, he dipped his tongue between her lips, then slid slowly into her moist heat in one long and erotically painful stroke. She arched against him and cried his name against his mouth, rattling what little control he had left with more force than the unstable thermal balance of a collapsing molecular protocloud.

Heaven didn't get any better than this.

And if he didn't maintain some control, it was going to be over before they both realized what had happened. He'd waited too long to have her in his arms, to have her writhing beneath him. He'd waited an eternity to see her green eyes filled with passion and heat while she called his name. He'd waited a lifetime for the magic between them to erupt…and he didn't want to have it end prematurely. He attempted to concentrate on logarithmic functions but failed when the only spontaneous developments that filtered through his mind had to do with the variety of ways he wanted to make love to the woman clinging to him.

Continuity and force equations meant nothing when she arched her back and cried his name. The force of her release, combined with the soft little moaning sounds she made as her body convulsed around him, shattered what was left of his control. A powerful wave of completion crashed through him, sending him over the edge and into the oblivion he'd only dreamed he'd find in the arms of the woman he loved.

SYDNEY ROLLED onto her side and reached for the extra pillow, not quite ready to begin her day. She had patients scheduled fifteen minutes apart from the time she opened the clinic until she closed at noon. For only being open three hours on Saturday, it was going to be a very long day.

Her hand came into contact with warm flesh. Warm *male* flesh.

Her eyes shot open.

Dear God, what had she done?

She sat upright, blinking several times. No. She couldn't have.

She looked down at the man sleeping peacefully beside her. Oh, but she had—*they* had. Not once, but three times during the most glorious night in her entire life.

She stared at him, unable to believe her eyes, unable to believe she'd actually made love to him. A part of her had hoped she'd been dreaming. An exquisite, deliciously wicked dream, but a dream nonetheless. But...it had been *real!*

She glanced at the bedside clock. She had to be at the clinic in an hour, and she needed to check and feed the puppies they'd rescued last night. Thank goodness she lived right behind her office. Still, she didn't have time for recriminations. Those would have to wait for later when she really had the time to beat herself up over doing something not only incredibly stupid, but monumentally careless.

She dropped her head into her hands. God, what had she been thinking? But she knew the answer to that question. Oh, that was the easy part. The hard part was why on earth had she let things go so far? Why hadn't she stopped him?

Because I needed to feel loved.

She pulled in a deep breath. She was asking for trouble if she started thinking in terms of love and forever.

She shook the thought from her mind. There was no such thing as love or forever. At least not for her. They were fine emotions for others, but she didn't believe in anything quite so frivolous.

She'd once foolishly believed in happily-ever-after, but had been disabused of that girlhood dream. When she'd left Kentucky, she'd sworn to herself that she'd never again be quite so impractical or naive.

She had more immediate problems at hand, such as how to get the heck out of her own bed without waking Derek.

She looked down at him again. His black hair fell over his forehead, his angled features were softened in sleep. He slept as if he hadn't a care in the world, with one arm flung carelessly over his head, the other draped across his lean, hard stomach. The floral sheet lay tangled around his trim waist, and his long legs hung off the edge of her bed. Until last night, she'd thought she'd known everything about him. Now she knew more than she'd ever dreamed possible.

Slowly, so she wouldn't wake him, she eased toward the edge of the bed. If she could shower, dress and sneak out before he woke, then she wouldn't have to face him until later. She knew he was leaving tomorrow for some scientists' convention in San Francisco, so maybe if she was really lucky, she wouldn't have to face Derek for several days. Maybe by that time she'd have come up with a reasonable excuse as to why she'd slept with him in the first place.

But she already knew the answer. She'd needed someone and Derek had been there for her, just as she'd expected him to be, just as he always had been. Losing that dam had filled her with doubt about her decision to have a child.

She lowered her feet to the floor and quietly

reached for her robe. The bed jostled and she held her breath. She chanced a peek over her shoulder, and let out the breath she'd been holding when she found him still sound asleep. Carefully, she left the bed, snagged her robe and tiptoed into the bathroom.

By the time she finished with her shower, she still hadn't come to terms with what she'd done with Derek during the dark hours of the night. Worse, she'd never imagined making love to him would make her feel so…complete.

Quietly, she opened the door and peered into the bedroom. The bed was deserted. Maybe he'd left while she was in the shower. Maybe he'd realized what a huge mistake they'd made and had sneaked away while she was otherwise occupied. She crept across the cold hardwood floor to the window. Her heart sank. Derek's Explorer was still parked beside her Jeep. God, she didn't want to face him this morning. She needed time to regain her composure. She needed time to find the words to tell him they'd made a huge mistake—a mistake that could have lasting effects considering they hadn't used any protection.

She couldn't think about that now. Right now she had to get through the next thirty minutes. She'd think about the repercussions of what had transpired between them later—like in about five or six days when Derek returned from his Trekkie convention.

She dressed quickly in a pair of jeans and her favorite I've Gone to the Dogs sweatshirt. As she slipped her feet into the battered sneakers she always wore to the clinic, Derek strolled into the bedroom with two mugs of coffee clutched in his hands. Her fingers stilled over the laces as she looked up at him. Eyes as blue as sapphires pierced her. They weren't cold like most jewels, but warm and held a tenderness she didn't want to think about.

He wore only a pair of jeans, his magnificent upper body bare. She'd kissed that chest only hours before, had plied her fingers through the rich black sprinkling of hair. She'd used her tongue to trace the thin line of hair that ran down his flat, hard stomach and disappeared into the jeans he wore now. She'd loved every inch of his body during the early hours of the morning. He'd made her feel loved and cherished and had turned her inside out with need and desire. And she'd been too selfish to stop him. She'd wanted him and he'd returned that need with a ferocity that had taken her to new heights.

"Good morning," he said, his voice rough and scratchy from sleep. He handed her one of the mugs and planted a quick hard kiss on her lips. "Since when did you start drinking decaf?"

He sat beside her, and his warm male scent overwhelmed her. She had a wild urge to close the clinic and stay right in this room with him for the remainder of the day, consequences be damned.

"This week," she answered, setting the mug on the nightstand. She finished tying her sneakers and left the bed and temptation. This was not good. They couldn't have a repeat performance, and she fought to ignore her body's response to his nearness.

She grabbed the brush off her dresser and ran it through her hair. The gold clip she usually wore to hold her curls in place while she worked wasn't where she kept it. Then she remembered that it was probably lying on the floor somewhere in her office, where Derek had tossed it last night. Using a scrunchie, she pulled her hair into a ponytail.

"I've got to run," she said, not looking at him.

"Wanna try taking in a movie tonight?" he asked.

She started across the bedroom and stilled. It would be just like Derek to think that nothing had changed between them. But it had. There'd be no more movies together. No more of him helping her remodel the veterinary clinic on Sunday afternoons, or her helping him with yard work or listening to his excitement at some new discovery he'd made at the lab. There'd be no more just hanging out together because they enjoyed each other's company. Their relationship had been irrevocably changed, and that saddened her. By making love to him, she may have very well destroyed the one thing that had always mattered to her—his friendship.

She turned and pasted on a smile she really didn't feel. "I can't. I shouldn't be away from those puppies for too long. Lock up when you leave, okay?"

She grabbed her purse off the chair and hurried out of the bedroom. She nearly made it to the front door when she heard his voice behind her.

"Syd?"

Her hand stilled over the knob, but she

couldn't face him. She felt him behind her, his nearness, his heat. His hands settled on her shoulders and he gently turned her around.

She stared at his chest, and her hands itched to touch him. "Look, Derek...I—"

"Sh," he whispered, then gently lifted her chin until she had no choice but to look into his sexier than sin eyes. Why hadn't she noticed how incredibly sexy he was before now?

Before she could guess his intent, he ducked his head and settled his lips over hers. She expected a gentle goodbye kiss, but he was surprisingly demanding, his tongue slipping expertly between her lips to tangle with hers. And God help her, she responded to him with equal hunger, slipping her arms around his neck to hold him close. This was not the way to put an end to a relationship before things became even more complicated. But her breasts ached and felt heavy. Heat balled in her tummy then burst through her. When his hands skimmed down her spine and settled on her hips, she arched toward him. Her mind might be telling her he was off-limits, but her body had something much more pleasurable in mind.

He lifted his head and she looked up at him. A wicked grin curved his lips. She felt dazed and more alive than she could recall, both at the same time.

He ran his thumb over her lips, then kissed her quick. "I'll call you later," he said. Was his voice really filled with sexual intent, or was that just her overactive imagination?

She couldn't speak. She couldn't have found

her voice with two hands and a road map. Pulling her arms from around his neck, she reached behind her and opened the door, then slipped out into the bright Saturday morning sunshine.

As she crossed the lawn toward the clinic, she wondered what on earth she was going to do when she made the return visit to the gynecologist next week for her pregnancy test. He'd told her the chances were good that she'd be pregnant, but last night she'd increased the odds tenfold.

But she had a bigger problem. If she did learn she was pregnant, who was the father? The daddy-to-go she'd bought and paid for, or the man who'd just kissed her senseless?

"THANK YOU, Dr. Travers." Mrs. Cushing scooped her beloved, multichampioned Scottish terrier into her arms. "Freezing Fergus's sperm was a brilliant idea. I can't thank you enough." The elderly woman hugged her pet close. "These puppies will be worth a fortune!"

Sydney hid a self-conscious grin. Maggie wasn't the only one pregnant. She'd received confirmation that morning from her gynecologist. She was indeed going to have a baby. And while she was thrilled at the prospect, she had to find a way to tell Derek that he might or might not be the father.

"Now that we know she's in whelp, bring her back in five weeks." Sydney jotted a few health notes on Maggie's chart, then looked up at Mrs. Cushing. "I'd like to do an ultrasound to see how many pups to expect."

"Let's hope for a good-size litter," Mrs. Cushing said. "I've got deposits on four puppies already."

Sydney grinned at the enterprising woman and gave Maggie one last pat on the head before leading the pair out of the examination room. "See you in five weeks."

She made a final note on the chart, then handed it to her assistant, Rachel.

"Who's up next?" she asked, checking her watch. She was supposed to meet Derek for dinner at their favorite Mexican restaurant in an hour. With any luck at all, the place would be packed. Considering the announcement she planned, the larger the crowd, the safer she'd feel.

"Derek Buchanan in exam two." Rachel pushed her glasses up the bridge of her nose and handed her a chart. "Bronson got into a fight with his neighbor's Siamese cat again. Chester three, Bronson zero."

Sydney's stomach sank. She wasn't ready to see him. Suddenly, the week he'd been away at his convention hardly seemed long enough her for to prepare her little speech. Wasn't she supposed to have another hour until her time was up and she had to tell him the most glorious night she'd ever experienced may or may not have resulted in the child she was carrying? She just wasn't ready. Not yet. Heck, maybe not ever, she thought.

"Bronson has a pretty nasty gash this time," Rachel said, then turned on the answering machine.

Any creature within a three-block radius who wasn't smart enough to avoid the ill-tempered

Chester failed to walk away unscathed. Derek's oversize lapdog was no exception.

"Is that it for the day?" Sydney asked, hopeful that she'd have at least another two or three patients so she could regain her hour reprieve.

"That should cover it." Rachel reached under the counter and grabbed her purse. "I've got a PTA meeting, so I can't stay."

"No problem. Derek knows the drill." Sydney flipped open Bronson's chart to make sure his vaccinations were current. "I'll see you in the morning."

Rachel headed toward the door. "You've got a spay, a neuter and a litter of bulldogs to deliver by C-section first thing tomorrow," she said over her shoulder. "Oh, and Frank Pritchard called. He wants to know if you could prescribe some vitamins for his daughter's goat. He didn't think you'd want the beast in the office after what happened the last time, so he'll stop by on his way to work tomorrow."

The last time Frank Pritchard's goat had been in her office, he'd managed to chew the vinyl chairs, kick Mrs. Garber's German shepherd, and butt Frank Pritchard hard enough to nearly send him over the counter. Willie was a sweet goat, as far as goats were concerned, but he tended to create havoc wherever he went.

With a final wave to Rachel, Sydney had no choice but to face Derek and see what sort of damage Chester had done to poor Bronson this time.

"Hi, Doc." Derek's blue eyes twinkled as he looked her up and down. A shiver passed through her as if he'd physically touched her.

"Hi, yourself," she said, trying to ignore the

way he made her body come alive with a simple look. The tightening of her breasts told her she failed miserably.

"You mistreating your dog again, Professor?"

"Millie's cat holds a grudge," he said good-naturedly. With little effort, he hefted Bronson onto the exam table. The sleeves of his cotton polo shirt stretched over biceps that Mr. America would envy. He might be a scientist, but he had the kind of body most women fantasized about, and she was no different. Since they'd made love she'd found herself doing some pretty heavy-duty fantasizing.

She dropped the chart on the counter and patted Bronson's thick back. "Hiya fella," she said, trying to concentrate on the dog.

The oversize Doberman whined, then turned his head to nuzzle her hand. Chester had managed to put a three-inch gash in Bronson's muzzle. "He's going to need stitches," she said, rubbing the dog's neck.

Derek sighed. "I had a feeling." He scratched the big red Dobie behind the ear affectionately. "You're in good hands, old boy. I told you Syd would take care of you."

Bronson's stubby tail wagged slightly.

"Want a hand?" Derek asked.

"Sure." Sydney finished her exam, then gathered the supplies she needed to sedate Bronson before sewing him back together.

Derek lifted the dog and carried him across the hall to the surgery. Sydney had missed him this week, and that bothered her almost as much as anticipating his reaction when she told him about the baby.

"Hold his head," she instructed Derek once he'd settled the dog on the surgical table.

Derek cradled Bronson's head in his large hands while she injected the sedative. He talked in soft, soothing tones as if Bronson were a baby rather than a hundred-pound Doberman pinscher. When he'd brought the flea-infested, malnourished pup to Sydney several months ago, it had the worst case of coccidiosis she'd ever treated. She hadn't been sure he'd make it, but to her surprise, the pup survived. Derek had adopted him, named him after Charles Bronson, and the pair became inseparable. Wherever Derek happened to be, Bronson could usually be found dozing nearby.

Once the dog was under the anaesthetic, she set about cleansing the wound. Twelve stitches later, Bronson's muzzle was repaired.

She stepped back to admire her handiwork, then covered the stitches with a salve. "Try to keep him out of trouble," she instructed, knowing the dog's penchant for mischief. Turning, she picked up the chart and jotted a few notes. "And be sure to remove the stitches in ten days."

Derek slipped up behind her and pulled her against him. He dipped his head and nuzzled, placing light, teasing kisses along the back of her neck. A shiver chased down her spine and the chart slipped from her fingers and clattered to the floor.

"I've been waiting all week to do that." He spun her around to face him. "And this," he murmured, before capturing her lips in a slow, drugging kiss that made her knees buckle.

Despite repeatedly telling herself all week long

that any relationship between them other than friendship was out of the question, she wreathed her arms around his neck and pressed her body to his.

"God, I've missed you, Syd," he said when he lifted his head.

Sydney's tummy did a flip at the honesty in his declaration. She tried to focus on what she had to tell him and not the guilt that had been her constant companion since she'd hurried out of the cottage Saturday morning.

She nodded, because she couldn't speak around the lump the size of a boulder clogging her throat, and stepped out of Derek's warm embrace. Picking up Bronson's chart, she wrote down a prescription for antibiotics, then turned to gather her instruments.

"Syd?" He stood behind her and placed a hand on her shoulder. "Sweetheart, what's wrong?" Concern filled his deep, clear voice, causing her heart to clench.

She shrugged his hand off, then stooped to pick up the wrapper for the cat gut she'd used to sew Bronson's muzzle. "Nothing."

Derek chuckled, the sound warm and welcoming. "I know you, remember?"

Sydney straightened and sighed, looking at her friend, and the possible father of her child. She tossed the torn wrapping in the wastebasket, then propped her backside against the metal table where Bronson still slept. "What would you say if I told you I wanted to have a baby?"

He crossed his arms over his lumberjack-size chest and gave her a teasing look. "I'd ask when you want to start rehearsals."

Syd sighed again and pushed away from the table. "Never mind." She left the room and headed toward the supply cabinet for the antibiotic salve for Bronson. She couldn't tell him, at least not yet.

She turned and nearly smacked into the firm wall of Derek's chest. His hands clamped onto her shoulders. "Are you pregnant?" he asked slowly.

Sydney swallowed. Why was it so hard to tell him? They were friends, and she had to remember that. Derek had never judged her, not once in her life, but she feared he would do so now once she told him the entire truth. She needed him to be that man she depended on as her friend.

And lover, her conscience jeered.

"Syd? What's going on?" he asked, his voice rough with emotion.

She looked into his eyes. They were curious, not hard and uncompromising as she'd imagined. His lips weren't drawn into a thin, tight line, but they would be when she told him everything. She couldn't bear it if she lost his friendship, but perhaps she already had. Perhaps they'd tossed away more than twenty years of friendship when they'd made love.

Sydney took a couple of steps back to garner courage. "Yes," she whispered, then watched a slow smile spread across his handsome face until he was grinning like the village idiot.

He might be grinning like a fool now, she thought. But when she finished telling him the entire story, he'd wish he'd never met her.

4

TOO MANY EMOTIONS to catalogue swept through Derek, but one continued to rise to the surface—pure, unadulterated joy.

A baby!

He and Syd had made a baby together.

Life didn't get much better than this, as far as he was concerned.

He wanted to pull her into his arms and hold her close. He wanted to kiss her senseless. He wanted to tell her how thrilled he was that such a special night had created a beautiful, wonderful miracle for them to cherish for the rest of their lives. He wanted to tell her how much he loved her.

The nervousness in her averted gaze kept him from making the declarations residing on the tip of his tongue.

"Are you sure?" he asked cautiously when she still wouldn't look at him.

She let out a puff of breath that feathered her wispy bangs across her forehead. "Oh, yeah. Real sure."

Her voice held more resignation than he would have liked considering her joyous news. "So soon?"

She stuffed her hands into her white lab coat,

but not before he noticed that they were trembling. "You'd be amazed at the strides medical science has made the last hundred years."

Her attempt at humor failed, due mainly to the nervousness in her voice. Something wasn't right. In fact, something was very wrong, and he hoped Syd wasn't angry with him. He hadn't taken steps to protect her, but how could they be sorry when their coming together had created something as beautiful as a child? A child made from love, to his way of thinking.

"Syd, are you happy about this?" he asked carefully, hoping.

She shifted her gaze to him, then back to the speckled linoleum. "That part gets a little tricky."

Alarm bells rang in his head. "What do you mean 'tricky'?"

She pulled in a deep breath, then met his gaze. Fear flashed momentarily across her features. "I mean..." She looked up at the ceiling and sucked in another breath, letting it out slowly. When she brought her gaze back to his, guilt filled her eyes, causing his heart to thud painfully with apprehension.

"Derek...I...well, you see..."

He crossed the space separating them and settled his hands on her shoulders. "What is it, Syd? What's going on?"

"I'm not sure if you're the father," she said in a rush. She stepped away, and his hands fell slowly to his sides as her statement registered.

"Not the father?" he repeated once the shock wore off. "How in the hell is that possible?"

"I'm sorry," she murmured, then slipped out of the room before he could stop her.

That was probably a good thing considering his earlier joy had been eclipsed by the red-hot anger bubbling up inside him.

Not the father?

He took several deep breaths, but they did little to calm the beast, the jealous beast, rearing its ugly head. Sydney was *his*. It was only right that this baby should be his, too. Okay, so he hadn't told her yet that she belonged to him, but after the night they'd spent together before he'd left town, he'd been pretty damned certain she knew exactly how he felt about her. Hadn't he made his feelings perfectly clear, *all night long?*

They'd had more than just sex. They'd made love, dammit.

He stepped into the now darkened corridor. The door to her office was open, the buttery glow of the desk lamp illuminating the shadowy passageway. The heels of his boots clicked along the tile as his long, angry stride ate up the distance. When he stepped into her office, the last thing he expected was to find her calmly sitting behind her desk reviewing a chart as if she hadn't just ripped out his heart and stomped all over it.

He propped his shoulder against the doorjamb and crossed his arms over his chest. "Who is he?" he demanded, his voice hard.

She shook her head, but refused to look at him. "No one. I mean, you're the only man I've had sex with."

"Last I heard, it takes two to make a baby."

She made a sound that resembled a laugh, but

he couldn't be sure. "Not necessarily," she said, tossing the chart on the inexpensive wood-grain desk.

He was becoming more confused, and irritated, by the minute. "What are you trying to say?"

She looked up at him, and he almost wished she hadn't. Guilt clouded her eyes, along with something else. Regret, maybe?

"I was artificially inseminated."

His world tilted, then slowly righted itself. She couldn't have surprised him more than if she'd claimed to have had sex with the entire Seattle Seahawks' offense.

"Good God, why on earth would you do a thing like that?"

Her chin lifted, a sign he knew all too well as a call to battle. "Because I wanted a baby," she said, her voice taking on a steely edge.

"When?"

"For a while now."

He shook his head. "No, when did you get..." God, if he couldn't even bring himself to say the words, how could he possibly hope to understand what had driven her to take such a drastic step?

"Inseminated?" she finished for him, her tone none the lighter. "The same day we...had sex."

The fact that she kept referring to their making love as "having sex" was beginning to grate on his nerves. No one was that good an actor. Something special had occurred that night, and great, mind-blowing sex didn't begin to scratch the surface of the emotions that had flowed so freely between them. They'd been too in tune with each other, too emotionally involved for that night to have been a fluke. Surely she didn't mean to write it off as an ultrafabulous one-night stand.

Derek pushed away from the door and dropped onto the sofa. With his feet braced apart, he settled his arms on his legs and scrubbed his hands down his face. "I don't believe this," he muttered.

She shoved a stack of files and charts away from the edge of the desk and gave him a steady look. "There's only a fifty-fifty chance the baby is yours." The tinge of regret in her voice gave him hope. Perhaps she really did want the baby to be his, but hadn't yet come to terms with her feelings.

"I don't expect anything from you," she continued slowly, as if choosing her words with care. "This is my baby, and I'm going to have it and raise it on my own. If we hadn't made... If we hadn't had sex, this discussion wouldn't even be taking place."

He had two choices. He could either ignore the fact that the kid might not be his, or he could capitalize on that fifty percent chance that he'd fathered Sydney's unborn baby.

Deciding the latter gave him more leverage in getting what he wanted—her—he wasn't above using a little underhanded strategy. He'd use whatever means at his disposal if it meant he could convince her they belonged together.

He stood and crossed the room. Her eyes widened as he closed the distance, then braced his hands on the arms of the worn leather chair, trapping her within his embrace. He leaned forward, intentionally surrounding her with a solid reminder of what they'd shared.

"There's a chance this baby is mine," he told her. "That's enough for me."

She tried to pull back, but he refused to allow her to escape, bending down until their lips were inches apart. He could feel her warm breath fan against his mouth, saw her eyes darken as he lightly brushed his lips against hers in a featherlight kiss meant to tantalize.

Oh yeah, he thought, as her mouth opened in silent invitation. It hadn't been a fluke. There was a connection, whether she was willing to admit it or not.

Instead of kissing her senseless the way his body demanded, he whispered, "Marry me."

Not exactly a romantic proposal, but then again, this wasn't exactly the conversation he'd expected, either.

She looked stunned. Her jaw fell slack, then she snapped her mouth closed and gave him a harsh glare. "Don't be ridiculous," she replied, a deep frown creasing her delicately arched eyebrows.

He straightened and glared down at her, trying like the devil to ignore the jab to his male ego. "Ridiculous? Syd, this entire conversation is ridiculous. First you tell me you're pregnant. Then you drop a bomb by telling me I might not be the father, but some…donor in a test tube could be. You tell me who's being ridiculous."

She stood and crossed her arms over her chest, then lifted her chin several notches. "I won't marry you," she said stubbornly. "You, or anyone. Ever."

"Why the hell not?" he demanded.

"I don't need to get married to have a child." She sidestepped him. "That was the whole point of artificial insemination."

"I'm not going to allow a child of mine to grow up without a father."

"This isn't the fifties, for crying out loud. There's no shame in being a single parent these days."

Old emotions he'd thought long forgotten rose to the surface. He'd been the product of single parenthood. Hell, he hadn't even known his father, so he knew firsthand how painful it could be for a kid growing up without a dad.

"Unwed motherhood may not carry the same stigma it did when I was born thirty years ago, but kids are cruel, Syd. Being labeled a bastard, even in this day and age, is going to hurt. I don't want my son or daughter facing the kind of cruelties I suffered."

"But you don't know that you *are* the father," she returned, attempting to reason with him.

"That's beside the point," he said, his patience slipping.

"That's the *entire* point." She turned her back on him as if to put an end to the conversation.

He came up behind her and laid his hands over her shoulders, gently using his thumbs to ease the tension knotting her neck. "You're wrong. You could be pregnant with my baby. You know I'll make you a good husband, Syd. Marry me."

She moved away, giving him no choice but to let her go. When she turned to face him, the moisture clouding her green eyes nearly had him pulling her back into his arms. The stubborn tilt of her chin kept him from following through.

"I won't marry you, Derek," she said with such firmness he nearly believed her. And he would have believed her, if there hadn't been a trace of longing mingled with confusion in her gaze.

Confusion he could handle. Confusion he could sway to his favor. How, he wasn't certain, but at least he had hope. For now, that was enough.

He placed his hands on his hips and gave her a cocksure grin he wasn't quite feeling, but his own stubbornness refused to allow her to see how much her rejection stung. "Care to bet on that, Doc?"

She arched an eyebrow, accepting his challenge in a way he found hard to resist. Who was he kidding? Everything about her was hard to resist.

"That sounds remarkably like a threat, Professor." His hopes climbed a notch at the slight waver in her voice.

"Sweetheart, it's a promise," he countered, hoping to keep her off balance.

He spun on his heel and strode toward the door. Pausing, he cast a look over his shoulder. "And for the record, Doc, we didn't just have sex. We made love."

A flash of desire flared in her eyes, seconds before worry pulled her eyebrows together in a frown. Her confusion caused a keen sense of male satisfaction to surge through him, despite the fact that he felt as if his life was beginning to unravel...and he didn't have a clue how to stop it.

AFTER SETTLING a still drowsy Bronson onto the large plaid doggie bed and reassuring himself the dog would be fine sleeping off the remnants of the mild anesthetic, Derek grabbed a lightweight jacket from the closet, then walked the short distance to The Wolf Den, a local bar and grill near the university. He'd never been much of a drinker, mainly because he had such a low tolerance for alcohol. But tonight he needed a drink, and maybe even a little male bonding. He needed something that would numb his mind and hopefully dull the sharp edges of pain surrounding his wounded heart. A little empathy from others of his species wouldn't hurt, either, and he was all for a cry-in-your-beer-country-song kind of night. And if a pretty coed wanted to hone her flirting skills with an old guy like himself, then who was he to argue? He had a case of injured male pride that could use a bit of salving.

He pulled open the heavy wooden door and nodded a greeting to the burly bouncer he recognized as a student he'd tutored in astronomy last term. Though the beefy-armed keeper of the peace looked like the type to incite a riot, the leather-sporting, Harley-loving Leonard had his sights set on a Ph.D. in philosophy. Somehow he couldn't quite picture Lenny quoting Sophocles or Descartes to a bunch of eager college freshmen, but then again, why not? If Sydney could get herself artificially inseminated then make love to him, both in the same day, then he figured just about anything was possible.

He sidled up to the bar and ordered a shot of Kessler's with a beer chaser from the young barmaid, then scanned the crowd looking for familiar faces. His gaze settled on a couple of students and a professor of economics he knew. When they waved him over, he didn't hesitate to join them.

Brad, the professor, pulled an empty chair up to the table for Derek. "Serious drinking tonight, eh Buchanan?"

"Damn serious," Derek agreed before tossing back the Kessler's in a move that would have made John Wayne proud. He suppressed a shudder as the amber whiskey burned down his throat and settled into his stomach like a ball of fire. Too late, he realized the Mexican dinner with Sydney had been skipped. He was operating on airplane food, and that sorry meal had been more than twelve hours ago. Drinking on an empty stomach probably would guarantee him the hangover from Hades, but numbness was his goal, and what better way to reach his destination than on the fast track.

He silently signaled for the waitress to bring him another whiskey; his vocal cords needed time to recover from the liquid inferno he'd just sucked down.

"Must be a woman," said Phil Butler, a twenty-two-year-old genius already accepted as a Ph.D. candidate in mathematics. Phil, with his sun-bleached hair and freckled complexion, looked as if he belonged in a fifties malt shop chasing poodle skirts rather than pounding back beers in a smoky bar with the Rolling Stones blaring on a Wurlitzer.

"Isn't it always?" Hank Robinson, the Huskies'

number-one draft pick, added before lifting a bottle of beer to his lips.

When the waitress delivered his Kessler's, Derek downed the second shot while using tavern sign language to order a round for his bonding buddies. "Every time," he rasped, relieved that his voice didn't squeak like a pubescent teen's from the abuse of the whiskey.

He set the shot glass on the square, black-lacquered table with a snap. "Why do women have to be so antithetic?" he asked, causing the trio of bachelors to laugh.

Derek didn't really expect an answer, but some insight into the female psyche might prove useful, especially since trying to understand what made his sexy veterinarian tick was near impossible.

What was wrong with marriage? Hell, what was wrong with marrying him? Couldn't the fool woman see he was in love with her?

"Let me guess," Brad said, balancing his chair on its rear legs. "She wants a little romance in her life."

Now it was Derek's turn to laugh. Romance? Sydney? "Hardly," he muttered, reaching for his beer. Roses and pretty words weren't for her, that much he knew. But he'd gladly give her all the romance she could handle, and then some, if she'd let him get close enough.

And that's what bothered him, he realized. She wouldn't let him, or anyone, get too close. Oh, sure, they'd been plenty close the night they'd made love, but once she slipped from beneath the sheets, a wall had gone up around her, and he hadn't realized it until now.

The waitress returned with a round of beers, and Derek laid a twenty on the table. When he waved away his change, she smiled her thanks, one of those warm, sultry smiles that should have soothed the ruffled feathers of his ego, but surprisingly did nothing for him.

Hank braced his enormous forearms on the table and cradled the fresh bottle of beer between his hands. "I'll bet she's saying you're not supportive enough of her goals," he suggested, his black-as-midnight eyes locked on the waitress's denim-clad behind.

Through the Kessler fog clouding his brain, Derek tried to concentrate on Sydney's goals. He frowned. Maybe Hank was right. He hadn't been very supportive of her grand plan of artificial insemination. In fact, he'd been downright offended. How was a man supposed to feel knowing he could be so easily replaced?

"I'm supportive," he grumbled, with a dose of apprehension. He *was* supportive of her decision to have the baby, just not of her plan to raise his kid without him.

Phil finished off the last of his beer, then reached for the fresh bottle. "I bet she says you don't understand her needs."

Derek leaned back into the chair, laced his fingers together and placed them behind his head. "I thought I did," he admitted after careful consideration. Obviously, he'd been wrong on that score, too.

Damn, he thought. He just couldn't win. If anyone was keeping score, he'd be in the hole and buried by now.

Brad considered him over the rim of his beer bottle. "Maybe you don't listen to her," he said, tipping the edge of the bottle toward him to emphasize his point. "I bet she wants to 'communicate' instead of having sex all the time."

Derek straightened. They didn't have sex all the time! It had only been one night. And it wasn't sex—they made love.

"I communicate just fine. In fact, she knows exactly how I feel." He'd made certain of that when he'd left her office tonight.

Hank reached into the bowl of warmed peanuts. "Buy her roses." He cracked open the shell and popped the nut into his mouth. "Women love flowers," he offered helpfully.

Phil nodded in agreement. "Then take her to see some chick flick and just hold her hand. Chicks get off on that romantic stuff."

"How about a romantic dinner?" Brad interjected. "Then, just kiss her at the door. No sex for, say, oh…at least a week."

Derek shook his head and closed his eyes, but promptly snapped them open again when the room started to spin. "You guys are a lot of help," he said, unsure if sarcasm had any effect when your words were starting to slur.

"What's the problem, Buchanan? She dump you?" Brad asked, his voice suddenly filled with sympathy.

That's what he wanted. Sympathy. He wanted his buddies, his own breed, someone he could connect with on a gender-to-gender level to commiserate with him. But there was only so much sympathy a guy could garner without being called a sissy, and he wasn't about to reveal that he'd been replaced by a frozen pop.

He thought about Brad's question a minute longer. "No," he finally said, then leaned forward and braced his arms on the table. "I don't think it's possible to get dumped when we never really had an official this-goes-in-the-books relationship."

He wasn't about to let on that one night of awesome sex quite possibly was the only qualifier to a relationship with Syd. They'd have a field day with him if they knew he'd been mooning after some woman for months. He didn't think he was that pathetic, but he wasn't about to risk his male pride twice in the same night.

"She wants to get serious and you're determined to hold on to your freedom," Phil said, then tossed a peanut into his mouth. "Fear of commitment. Happens all the time. Women hit a certain age and all they can think about is diamond rings and white dresses."

Hank tossed an empty peanut shell at Phil. "Like you'd know, Egbert," Hank said, laughing. "When did you ever have a serious relationship? You just escaped puberty—what—two years ago?"

"She's pregnant," Derek blurted. He didn't know why he added that truth, but blamed his loosened tongue on the alcohol.

A collective groan sounded around the table from his male *compadres*.

Phil leaned over and patted Derek on the back. "Goodbye freedom," he said.

"She won't marry me," he confessed. Hell, the only thing left unsaid was a declaration about the sperm donor. No more booze for him, he thought with a grimace, sliding the beer bottle toward the center of the table. He should take the stuff back to the lab and have it analyzed for truth serum. He was spilling his guts like an A.M. talk-radio caller.

"Ah," Brad said sympathetically. "An independent woman. That can be a problem."

"Can be a problem? She's making me crazy," Derek admitted. "She insists she can do everything on her own." *Including making her own babies, for crying out loud.*

Phil signaled for the waitress, waving the empty bowl of peanuts in her direction. "She probably doesn't need you," the young Einstein reasoned.

"Yes she does," Derek argued. "She's just too damned stubborn to realize it." She'd been twisting him in knots for months. Why on earth should he think that would change just because they'd made love? This was, after all, Sydney Travers they were talking about.

"She *thinks* she doesn't need you," Brad clarified.

"And how in the world do you combat an attitude like that?"

Brad settled his chair back on all fours. "Show her she does."

Derek looked at his friend and co-worker. "Any suggestions?"

The professor shrugged. "I dunno. Do for her what she usually does for herself. If she's one of those independent types, you need to make her understand that she won't lose her identity if she depends on a man once in a while."

"Come on, Prof," Hank interrupted. "Do you really want to do that? I mean, giving up your freedom for some broad." The hulking football player shuddered with mock revulsion.

Derek leveled his gaze on the 250-pound offensive lineman. "She's not some broad, Robinson," he said with enough threat in his voice to make Hank realize that the guy who'd exuded untold patience in getting him through a basic physics class wouldn't hesitate to take him outside and use him to wipe up the parking lot. "She's going to be the mother of my child."

Well, it may be my child, he added silently.

By the time the waitress delivered fresh peanuts and cleared away the empty beer bottles, Derek had a plan forming in his befuddled mind and didn't hesitate to ask her for extra napkins and a pen.

He started by drawing lines on one of the napkins.

"What are you doing?" Brad asked. Hank and Phil moved in closer to get a better look.

"What's the basic principle of any scientific experiment?" Derek asked them, his concentration on the sketchy charts and graphs.

"You can't approach romance like an experiment," Hank warned.

"Yes, I can," Derek said, jotting notes and formulas on another napkin. "Come on. What's the basic principle?"

"The hypothesis," Phil answered.

"Good." Derek continued making notes on another napkin.

"You can't be serious about this, Derek," Brad said in an attempt to discourage him. "You want to win her over, not dissect her like some lab rat."

"Trust me. I'll make it work," he said to Brad, then glanced at Phil. "What follows the hypothesis?"

Phil let out a huff of breath. "Develop the necessary questions that will lead you to the appropriate conclusions."

Derek grinned. "Exactly."

Phil scratched his head. "You lost me, Professor."

"It's simple," Derek said, once again filled with confidence that he could win the heart of the woman he loved. "All I have to do is lead her to the right conclusion."

"Which is?" Brad asked in a voice filled with skepticism.

Derek laughed, and the tension he'd felt before arriving at The Wolf Den eased. "I'm going to bring her to the logical conclusion that she can't live without me."

The men sat quietly, lost in their own thoughts while the jukebox blared an old rock tune by Jim Morrison, coercing a woman to break on through to the other side.

"There's one problem with your plan, Professor," Phil said when the jukebox quieted. "Women just aren't logical."

5

BELLS.

Wedding bells?

Never.

No. Not ever. At least not for her.

Then why was she standing in front of a priest? Why was Rachel gently dabbing her eyes with a lace handkerchief? And why on earth was Derek grinning like a fool?

The bells continued to ring, growing louder and more threatening. She wanted to run. She tried to move, but something was tugging on her foot, keeping her rooted to the spot. She looked down and stared dumbfounded at the leg iron manacled around her ankle. She followed the thick, iron links of the chain leading to a large, black cast-iron ball attached to the other end....

Sydney's eyes shot open and she struggled for breath. Blood pounded in her ears, matching the rapid cadence of her heart. A shiver passed over her as the remnants of the nightmare passed, and she reached for the blankets twisted around her legs.

The ringing started again, and she stilled. Fear momentarily slammed into her, until she recognized the sound—the doorbell. Letting out a shaky breath, she untangled her feet and snagged her robe from the nearby Victorian chair she'd bought at a yard sale for a song.

She peered out the window and instantly recognized Derek's Explorer parked beside her Jeep. After the way they'd parted two days ago, she hadn't really expected him to show up for their standing weekly breakfast. For all of two seconds she considered crawling back into bed and pulling the covers over her head. She'd have to face him sooner or later. She preferred later, but from the insistent ringing of the bell, later wasn't going to be an option.

Shrugging into her robe, she hurried down the hall to the front door, telling herself that the odd stirring in her tummy wasn't dread, but relief. Relief that she hadn't lost her best friend despite her horrendous lack of judgment and total loss of common sense when she'd slipped between the sheets for one night of incredibly hot sex.

She opened the door and her breath caught in her throat. His eyes held something that had the power to turn her blood to ice—tenderness, and worse, love.

Stop being so silly, she chastised herself as she struggled to pull valuable oxygen into her lungs. She didn't believe in love. She was only suffering from the remnants of her nightmare. Besides, how could something exist if she didn't believe in it in the first place?

"Good morning," he said, handing her the Sunday paper.

The smile she gave him was weak at best. "Good morning," she managed to reply, a little stunned by the emotions invading her heart. *Hor-*

mones, she reasoned, opening the door wider. *Not emotions!*

His answering grin was warm and held none of the animosity she'd spent the past thirty-six hours imagining. He stepped through the door, planted a quick, hard kiss on her lips, then strolled into the kitchen, Bronson following close behind.

"No coffee?" Derek asked, untying the pink bakery box and setting it on the table.

"I slept late." She tried to ignore the sparks of awareness that had flared to life when his lips touched hers. No passing those off as hormones, she thought, unless lust qualified.

She followed him into the kitchen. "I didn't expect you."

He still had that tender grin on his handsome face when he turned toward her. Gently, he lifted his hand and cupped her cheek in his palm. The warmth in his eyes matched his touch, and his gaze traveled over her face. Searching? she wondered. But for what? The truth that she was thrilled to see him even though she'd turned down his proposal of marriage?

She thought he was going to kiss her again. Against her will, her body hummed in anticipation and she lifted her face toward his.

"And miss breakfast with my favorite vet?" He dropped his hand and turned his attention to the coffeepot. The loss of heat, along with a stab of disappointment that he wasn't going to kiss her, made her frown.

Hormones.

Except she had a very bad feeling she was lying to herself.

She propped her shoulder against the doorjamb and watched Derek make himself at home, as he always did, in her compact kitchen. He grabbed the carafe and filled it with water. Longing swept over her in an unexpected rush as she watched the play of muscle beneath the thin material of his tan, cotton shirt. The fabric pulled tight across his wide shoulders when he reached into the cabinet for the coffee and filters.

Her knees went weak.

After their up-close-and-personal encounter, she knew how smooth his hard flesh would feel against her hands, how his flesh would quiver and jump beneath her touch.

He turned to take two mugs out of the cabinet. She swallowed hard, and her gaze dipped to the open collar of his shirt, zeroing in on the dark sprinkling of chest hair. She knew how his wide chest would feel pressed against her breasts, how the hair on his chest would tease her breasts as he covered her with his body.

She nearly groaned with wanting when she thought of how his thick, muscled thighs would feel as he moved rhythmically against her, taking her to the heights of...

She let out a puff of breath, cinched the belt of her robe tight, then shoved her hands into her pockets. She fought her desire to run her fingers over that hard, smooth flesh and beg him to take her to bed.

"I need to change," she said. Wearing nothing beneath her robe but an oversize T-shirt was just too tempting, considering she couldn't stop thinking about bodies touching in the most intimate ways possible.

He glanced over his shoulder at her, a wicked gleam in his eyes that stirred her already overactive senses. "You look fine to me."

She didn't have an answer for that. "I'll be right back," she murmured, then hurried down the hall to the safety of her bedroom.

After a fast—and very cold—shower, she dressed in a pair of faded jeans and an old flannel shirt. She had to wear something she wouldn't worry about ruining, since she planned to paint the cabinets in the reception area of the office today. Satisfied she looked non-sexy enough to keep her mind on things other than what she really wanted to do with Derek, she returned to the kitchen.

He sat at the table, one booted foot resting on his knee, his nose buried in the sports section of the Sunday paper. Bronson lay curled beneath the table, patiently waiting for treats. As she poured herself a cup of decaf, the little domestic scene took on a life of its own. She envisioned a dark-haired baby with blue eyes cradled in Derek's strong arms. In her fantasy, Derek looked up at her, his eyes filled with tenderness as he said, "Thank you."

She shook her head to clear the image. She didn't know if the baby was Derek's or not. He claimed it didn't matter, but she knew better. It would matter one day, and that was something she couldn't bear to see happen. Besides, this was *her* baby, and they didn't need a man in their lives. Wasn't that the point in choosing to have a child on her own?

She carried her coffee to the table and sat, reaching for the life-style section of the paper. She wanted to ask him why he was behaving as if this were any other Sunday morning. What kind of game was he playing? How could he pretend their relationship hadn't changed? She'd slept with him, and he'd been right, they hadn't had sex, they'd made love. That fact frightened her almost as much as her uninhibited response. She'd lost herself to him completely, something she'd never experienced, until Derek. He'd shown her that passion capable of setting her soul on fire did indeed exist. He even had her thinking about silly notions, such as love and happily-ever-after. She'd never felt so totally in tune with another human being.

Until Derek.

Their relationship had been irrevocably altered. She'd thrown his marriage proposal back in his face. She'd told him she was pregnant. She'd admitted she didn't know who the father was...and yet here he was, reading the sports section, drinking coffee and slipping Bronson blueberry muffin scraps as if nothing were out of the ordinary.

He traded the sports section for the comics. She wanted to scream with frustration.

"So what's on the agenda for today, Doc?"

Erotic images filtered through her mind, and her hand stilled as she reached into the bakery box for a bagel. She cleared her throat. "I was planning to paint the cabinets in the reception area. I primed them last week," she said, refusing to look at him just in case her thoughts were evident in her eyes.

"I don't think that's a good idea." The authoritative note in his voice had her lifting her gaze to his. A frown creased his brow. "The paint fumes can't be good for the baby."

She dropped the bagel on her plate, feeling a sense of satisfaction when his frown deepened. "I appreciate your concern, but it's not necessary." She didn't mean to sound quite so snippy, but she didn't like the idea of anyone telling her what to do. And she didn't care one iota for the proprietary tone in his voice.

His brows drew closer together. "Unnecessary, or unwanted?"

"Both," she stated honestly. "Look, I know you're concerned, but—"

"You bet I'm concerned." Irritation flashed in his eyes as he set the comics aside. "That's my baby you're carrying."

"You don't know that," she said defensively. Were they destined to argue every time they saw each other now? A part of her wished she could take back that night; another part of her wished for an instant replay.

"Neither do you." The hardness in his voice matched his granite stare. This was a side of Derek she'd never seen and wasn't sure she liked. He'd always been so easygoing, taking the ups and downs of life with a grain of salt.

She sighed, hating that she'd done this to him, and wished they could just go on as they always had. "Derek, I don't want to argue."

He shoved his hand through his thick black hair in an impatient gesture. "How long are you going to avoid the truth? Sooner or later you're going to have to face the fact that we're going to have a baby."

She pushed away from the table and stood. "*I'm* going to have a baby. You don't know that it's yours."

His face shifted into a scowl. "Do you really think that matters to me? As far as I'm concerned, this is my kid, too."

She had to be insane. Any other woman would have jumped for joy to have a sweet, wonderful and caring man like Derek insisting that the child she was carrying was his. But not her. Oh no, she'd rather make both of their lives miserable. "It does matter," she finally said.

She slipped out the back door and followed the path to the small, concrete patio because she couldn't bear to see the hurt in his eyes. Hurt she'd put there, and would do so again and again until he realized she wasn't going to budge in her decision to have this child on her own.

Seconds later she heard the squeak of the screen door, followed by the click of his boots on the cobblestones. She kept her back to him, hoping he'd take the hint and leave her alone with her guilt. No such luck, she thought, when his arms slipped around her and he pulled her against him. He placed a light kiss against her neck. A shiver chased down her spine.

"Syd, you're wrong." His voice was soft and deep and caused a delicious pressure to tighten in her belly. "It doesn't matter. Not to me."

She turned in his arms. His eyes were filled with patience and understanding, causing her guilt to triple. "It matters to me."

He shifted his hands to cup her face gently between his palms. His mouth tipped into a smile that warmed her to her toes. "When are you going to get it through that thick head of yours that I love you? You're what matters to me, Syd."

Ever so slowly, as if he feared she'd bolt from his arms, he dipped his head. "Only you," he whispered, then captured her lips in a kiss so tender it nearly made her weep.

She couldn't love Derek. She wouldn't love him. At least not the way he wanted, expected and deserved. She'd taken that path once and the road had been fraught with lies and deceit. And pain. The crushing blow that had prompted her return to Seattle came rushing back, pounding through her conscience with the same clarity as when she'd first learned she'd been cast in the role of fool.

Before she gave in to the feelings Derek was so competently stirring inside her, she pulled away. "You're crazy," she said, her voice catching.

His eyes darkened. "About you." The familiar and all too sexy rumble of his voice skirted along her nerve endings.

"Derek—"

"I've been thinking," he said quickly, stilling the warning she'd been about to issue.

Dropping onto a floral, cushioned patio chair, she pulled her knees to her chest and wrapped her arms around her legs. "Uh-oh," she muttered. "Now we're in trouble."

He crossed his arms over his chest and gave her a tolerant look. "Would you hear me out?"

Aiming for a lightheartedness she was far from feeling, she asked, "Do I have to?"

"Yeah, you do." The barest hint of a smile played around his eyes as he spun the other chair around to face her, and sat. Leaning forward, he braced his elbows on his knees and looked at her. "It makes a lot of sense for us to get married."

Her shoulders slumped. Why wouldn't he drop this wild idea of marriage? "Why would you want to saddle yourself with a pregnant wife and a kid that might not even be yours?"

"Stop arguing long enough to hear me out." The patience in his voice surprised her, along with his tenacity. What ever happened to go-with-the-flow Professor Marshmallow?

"I'm listening." She rested her chin on her raised knees, arguments at the ready.

He reached into the pocket of his shirt and produced a napkin covered with marks, graphs and symbols she didn't recognize. "Insurance," he said suddenly.

"Insurance?" she parroted.

He nodded and smiled. "Medical insurance. You do realize the costs involved in having a baby, don't you? There's the hospital, the obstetrician, the pediatrician," he said, using his fingers to tick off each costly item, "not to mention all those well-baby visits once the baby's born."

"Of all the…" *unromantic things to say*, she thought to herself. She straightened and gave him a disbelieving glare. "I have insurance, thank you."

"And I'll bet it's costing you a small fortune," he stated reasonably. "If we get married, you and the baby would be covered on my insurance through the university."

"That's hardly a reason to get married," she said, her voice infused with sarcasm.

He bent his head to consult the napkin again. A lock of dark hair fell over his brow. If she wasn't already irritated with him, she just might think he looked awfully adorable.

He tapped his finger against the napkin. "What about child care? Good child care runs a small fortune."

She shifted and tucked her legs beneath her. "You planning on quitting your job to stay home and take care of the baby?" She snapped her fingers. "Darn, there goes the free medical coverage."

He gave her another tolerant look that said she wasn't taking this at all seriously. "No, but I can afford to hire a good in-home child-care provider."

"I can afford it, too, Derek. I'm not exactly a pauper." The clinic was doing quite well, and it provided her with more than enough money to cover her day-to-day living expenses, with plenty left over at the end of each month for a healthy balance in her savings account. Tucked away in various investments was the proceeds from her parents' small estate and life insurance policies. She was hardly starving.

He consulted the napkin, shook his head, mumbled something she couldn't quite make out, then looked at her again. "Taxes."

"Taxes?"

"You're self-employed, Syd. The taxes have to be horrendous."

"What does that have to do with anything?" she asked, wondering if he was intentionally trying to insult her.

"Think of the tax breaks if we got married."

Her breath caught, then she laughed. He was serious! "Tax breaks?"

He grinned. He actually grinned at her.

"You don't want a wife," she said, feeling an unaccustomed sting to her feminine pride. "You want a tax deduction!"

"Of course I want a wife. Think of the money we could save with all the shared living expenses. You could sell this place and put the money away for the baby's college fund."

"I like my house just fine." It was hers, and no one could ever take it away from her. She'd never give up the security of owning her own home.

"It makes sense for you to move into my place. It's better suited for a family. And only one house means less lawn care and regular maintenance expenses for us to worry about."

She straightened and glared, but he was already consulting his damned list. "You don't do lawn care. You have a gardener. And do you even know what a hammer looks like?"

"Auto maintenance," he added.

"You want me to change your oil?" she asked incredulously.

"No," he said, chuckling. "That'd be my job."

He might be a brilliant scientist, he might be able to make even the most non-science-minded student understand the basic principles of physics or astronomy, but when it came to anything mechanical, Derek Buchanan, Ph.D., was the last person on earth she'd call for handyman services.

"You'd never have to worry about having a date for New Year's Eve," he said with an adoring smile that had her gnashing her teeth. "Or being alone on Valentine's Day, or your birthday, or—"

"Men," she muttered in exasperation, then swung her feet to the ground and stood.

His expression turned serious. "So? What do you think?"

Planting her hands on her hips, she bent forward to look squarely into his heavenly blue eyes. "I think you need your head examined," she snapped.

He had the audacity to look thoroughly confused. "What are you so upset about?"

"Ooh...never mind." She stepped past him and headed toward the house.

"Syd? Honey, what's wrong?"

She spun around and glared at him. "Don't you dare 'honey' me, you...*man*."

"I was only stating how practical—"

"The last thing a woman wants to hear is a laundry list of financial benefits in favor of matrimony!"

"But, I thought you wanted—"

She lifted her hand to stop him from saying another word. "Don't think, Derek. Please. Just don't think anymore, okay? My ego couldn't handle it."

She turned and stormed toward the house,

leaving Derek and his stupid napkin alone on the patio.

MYSTIFIED, Derek stared at the floral pattern on the lawn chair Sydney had vacated. He'd used logic. He'd stated every practical reason he could think of for why they should marry. The benefits far outweighed the risks.

Where had he gone wrong?

He rolled his shoulders in an attempt to ease the tension. He might have lost the first battle, but the war was far from over. His experiment had failed to produce the desired results, but he remained undaunted by what he viewed as a minor setback.

A stiff breeze stirred the leaves of the eucalyptus trees shading the house and tugged at the napkin in his hand. Stuffing it back in his pocket, he opted for a professional, rather than an emotional, analysis of the situation. A scientist understood that not all experiments were successful on the first attempt. Neil Armstrong wouldn't have walked on the moon and the *Eagle* never would have landed if the boys at NASA had gotten discouraged after a few setbacks. If Bell and Edison hadn't exhausted all avenues in the inventions of the telephone and the lightbulb, E-mail and microwave ovens would be nonexistent. In the name of science, he was determined to follow the tradition of the greatest scientific minds.

He stood and walked to the edge of the patio, wanting to give his subject time to cool off before he ventured back into the house to face her. He surveyed her backyard, noting the grass was in need of mowing. And she'd had the nerve to chastise him for hiring a gardener.

Why couldn't she see that marrying him was the best possible solution for them and for their child? Growing up without having a father around had been tough on him, especially once he'd started school. His mother had been great, and she'd done her best to make certain he'd never felt as if he missed out, but it just hadn't been the same.

He still remembered the confusion he felt the day he brought home a sign-up sheet from school for Indian Guides and she'd told him he wouldn't be allowed to join. Even when she said that the Indian Guides were strictly a father-and-son organization, he still hadn't understood. She'd attended every function he'd ever participated in; he just didn't see why this time was different. But she'd compensated, as she often did, by signing him up in the Cub Scouts, and even became an assistant den mother. Only it hadn't been the same. All his friends were Indian Guides. What hurt the most, however, was the realization that he was different from the other kids. Even the kids of divorced parents had dads. He didn't.

Didn't Sydney see the difficulties that lay ahead for her and their child? Surely she had to understand how being different when you were a kid was darn near the end of the world.

Women just aren't logical.

Phil's words echoed through his mind. The mathematical genius was only twenty-two years old. What did he know about women?

Based on Syd's reaction, plenty, he thought. In

the past few months, he'd listened to her talk about all her dates. He'd heard the tales, knew the flaws she saw in them all, whether real or imagined. She wasn't the flowers-and-pretty-words type, and she didn't play those silly mind games some women had down to a fine art. *Coy* was not in her vocabulary. She was a straightforward, no-frills kind of woman. With Sydney, there were no false pretenses. She was an honest woman who knew what she wanted and went after it with a vengeance.

Because I wanted a baby.

When?

For a while now.

He thrust his hands into the pockets of his trousers, frowning as that all-important snippet of conversation rattled around his mind.

"I don't believe it," he muttered when realization dawned. She hadn't been on a blood trail for a husband. She'd been searching for a sperm donor! And not the anonymous frozen pop she'd picked out at a clinic, but a live specimen.

His pride made him wonder if she'd made love to him to increase her chances of success, but that thought didn't last long. Sydney wasn't a manipulative woman. When they'd made love, her response had been honest. He'd touched her soul that night. Sydney loved him; she just didn't know it.

Yet.

Something was keeping her from committing to a relationship, but the reason for her staunch refusals bewildered him. Maybe if he knew why she was so against the institution of marriage, he'd have better luck overcoming her objections.

Since logic failed, it was time to exercise Plan B—once he judged the best approach for success.

And with Sydney, that wasn't going to be easy.

SYDNEY SAT cross-legged on the painter's tarp, Bronson's large muzzle resting on her knee. "Men are completely clueless," she complained to the dog, then dipped her paintbrush back into the gallon of peach semigloss. "I ought to give *him* a list—a list of reasons why he needs the help of a professional."

Bronson sighed in response, then closed his big, soulful eyes.

She angled her head and poked it inside the cabinet to paint the interior. "Insurance," she muttered. The idea was ludicrous. "Of all the asinine…"

Not that she'd accept a proposal of marriage in the first place, but he could have at least mentioned the special connection between them. Why couldn't he have tried to use their friendship and the camaraderie they shared as a reason for them to marry? If he'd told her he wanted a companion to share his life, she wouldn't have been half as insulted. Couldn't he have at least mentioned how compatible they were sexually? she thought in feminine outrage.

"Taxes," she grumbled. "What about desire?"

"Want a hand?"

She straightened, smacking her head on the cabinet. She glared at Derek over her shoulder and rubbed the sore spot on the back of her head. "You've done enough."

She refused to soften just because his sheepish grin bordered on rakish. Using her free hand, she tossed him a clean brush and indicated the cabinet doors set up on sawhorses in the waiting area, which she'd temporarily transformed into a construction site. "The doors need painting," she said, hoping Derek had wielded a paintbrush before.

She turned her attention back to her task, determined to ignore him. In taking his concern about paint fumes seriously, she'd opened the windows in the clinic. A warm breeze blew through the room, carrying the refreshing sea air of Puget Sound inside. The radio played softly in the background, the dial set on her favorite Seattle oldies station. Despite her earlier pique over Derek's emotionless proposal, for the first time in a week, she started to relax.

Bronson shifted and stood, groaning as he stretched his big red body. He stuck his wet nose against her cheek, wagged his stubby tail, then trotted away, probably to be near Derek.

"Hey there, pal." Derek's deep voice drifted to her on the warm breeze. "You been helping Syd?"

She tried to fight the grin tugging at her lips and failed. How could she stay angry with a guy who spoke with such affection to his dog?

Thirty minutes later, Derek breached the silence. "Hey, Syd?"

She shifted to the front of the next cabinet. Just

because she was softening, didn't mean she was ready to speak to him.

"Syd?" he called again.

She rolled her eyes. "What?"

"Did you eat anything?"

Her stomach grumbled in response. "No," she admitted, thinking of the abandoned bagel. She heard his exasperated sigh and grinned as she envisioned the white flag of surrender being raised, in the guise of food.

"How about a salad from the seafood place around the corner? My treat."

She looked up. He was leaning over the side of the counter, looking down at her, concern filling his direct gaze. What was it about this man, she wondered, that made her unable to remain angry with him for any length of time?

Because you know he'd never intentionally hurt you.

As much as she wanted to deny the truth, she couldn't. Derek would never lie to her, never make a fool out of her or lead her on with pretty phrases and promises he had no intention of keeping. His idea of romance might be more suited to a balance sheet, but he cared.

What was she thinking? She wasn't looking for romance. She'd learned a hard lesson that left her devastated, and she wasn't likely to forget the pain and humiliation she'd suffered.

A sharp gust of warm wind stirred the papers resting on the counter. She stood and eased the window down, leaving a small opening to allow the fresh air to flow through the area without creating havoc.

Turning back to Derek, she propped her elbows on the counter. "And a couple of those hard, crusty rolls?" she asked hopefully.

His answering grin was warm, and an unexpected flare of desire caught her off guard, as did the overwhelming urge to lean forward and press her lips against his. She nearly acted on the impulse...until a clatter and a yelp interrupted the awareness sparking between them.

Derek spun around and groaned. "Bronson, stay," he ordered, but the Dobie took off at a full run down the corridor to her office, leaving behind a trail of peach paw prints.

Sydney peered over the counter and cringed. The paint tray was overturned, the thick liquid oozing over the tarp. Derek pulled out the rag he'd stuffed into his back pocket and tried to staunch the flow, but there was too much paint. The semigloss oozed onto the linoleum in a large, slick pool of color.

Derek looked horrified.

She bit her lip to keep from laughing as she rounded the counter to the waiting area. "You see if Bronson's okay," she said, trying to keep a straight face. "I'll clean up."

She lifted the edge of the tarp and folded it back before more damage was done to the flooring, then covered the puddle with towels.

"Uh, Professor?" she called after him. She nodded toward his feet. "Take off your boots," she told him, struggling to keep the laughter out of her voice. "Or do you expect me to follow in your pretty peach footsteps?"

She smiled when he turned away in obvious

embarrassment. With some effort, he toed off his boots, careful not to track more paint through the clinic. As he disappeared down the corridor, following Bronson's paw prints, she hoped he didn't hear the giggles she could no longer contain.

6

UNSEASONABLY WARM weather caused by an early heat wave locked the northern Pacific Coast in record-setting June temperatures. Despite the sweltering heat, Sydney had no choice but to open the windows in the clinic, rather than make use of the new air-conditioning unit she'd had installed a few months ago. Unless of course she wanted her patients, their owners and her baby exposed to the lingering fumes of the bleach and turpentine Derek had employed to save the linoleum. Even the dozen or so pop-up pine air fresheners her assistant had scattered throughout the clinic did little to alleviate the strong chemical odors.

For two hours every day, the clinic was quiet, with no phone calls or patients, other than the occasional pet requiring twenty-four-hour care. She enjoyed the calm during the lunch break. It allowed her to keep up with whatever paperwork and unexpected emergencies arose during the morning hours. Occasionally, she'd slip away to the cottage to see to various household chores, or if weather permitted, yard work. Today, all she thought about was easing her tired body onto the sofa in her office and taking a nap.

Her last patient before the break, a depressed

Devon Rex with a penchant for chewing herself bald, still had her upset, and she wondered if the adrenaline rush sparked by her anger and frustration with the hardheaded cat owner was the cause of her sudden exhaustion. Then she recalled an article she'd read recently, warning her that her body might require extra sleep during pregnancy. As tempting as an afternoon snooze sounded, the responsibilities of running her own business outweighed that little noontime luxury.

Picking up the stack of charts she'd managed to complete despite the hectic morning, she walked to the front of the clinic to check her afternoon schedule. She found Rachel crouched on the floor, hanging the last of the cabinet doors.

"Can you believe these are already dry?" Rachel straightened and stood back to admire her handiwork.

"It's not surprising in this heat." Sydney set the charts in the wire basket. A dozen pink roses, artfully arranged in an elaborate cut-crystal vase, sat on the ledge above Rachel's desk, an anniversary surprise from her husband. Carefully, she tipped one of the buds and breathed in the intoxicating fragrance. "You should put these in the back fridge to keep them from wilting in this heat."

The phone rang, but since they were officially closed for two hours, Rachel allowed the answering machine to pick up. "I thought about it, but then I couldn't enjoy them."

Sydney felt a twinge of envy that even after eleven years, Rachel's husband was still interested enough to add a little romance to their marriage. No doubt Professor Practical would send her a high-yield, interest-bearing certificate of deposit for their anniversary.

But they weren't married, she reminded herself. And they weren't going to be, either. What she felt for Derek was friendship, and a major case of lust, nothing more.

"Besides," Rachel added, testing the hinge of the last cabinet door, "Steve's trying to make points because he had to pull duty on our anniversary weekend."

Steve was a career navy man, and Rachel didn't seem to mind the long absences sometimes required. They had a good marriage, which surprised Sydney considering Rachel and Steve had married a month after high school graduation. As far as Sydney knew, they were still crazy about each other, even though they'd married so young. The presence of Rachel's favorite pink roses stood as a testament to the affection still alive after more than a decade.

Rachel handed her the mail along with a few phone messages. "While you were discussing Tiffany's future on the show circuit with Davis Tompkins, I managed to sneak away to give the pups their noon feeding. That chubby little brindle had her eyes open."

Sydney smiled at Rachel's progress report on the pup that had stolen her assistant's heart. Despite being motherless, the litter she and Derek had saved were healthy and growing according to schedule. She'd been able to move them from the warmer a few days ago and into a large whelping box. She still hadn't decided what to do with the pups once they were old enough to go to homes, other than insist that the new owners bring them back for spaying and neutering, free of charge.

She smoothed the skirt of the cotton sundress she'd worn in hopes of keeping cool and comfortable, then eased onto the edge of the desk before flipping through the mail and scanning her messages. "Thank you for taking care of them for me, but you didn't have to do that," she said, telling herself she was not disappointed that Derek hadn't called her. After they'd cleaned up the paint spill yesterday, they'd shared a take-out lunch, then he'd driven Bronson home. She'd expected him to return with another ploy in convincing her to marry him, but surprisingly, she'd not heard from him.

She wasn't disappointed.

Really, she wasn't.

"I don't mind." Rachel sat on the floor to give the hinge a few good turns of the screwdriver, then checked the alignment again. "Besides, I couldn't stand to listen to another minute of poor Tiffany's howling."

Sydney sighed, thinking of the physical and emotional condition of the wooly-coated Devon Rex. "That man doesn't deserve to own a cat," she complained. "He had the nerve to ask me to prescribe Tiffany tranquilizers for the show."

Rachel laughed. "Show? With that peekaboo coat she's got going? I think not."

"He's determined she'll have her grand championship title at the next show," she said in disgust. She had nothing against showing animals, and even had a few clients ask her if she would conduct classes for amateurs interested in handling their own pets, but when the rigors of show life produced ill effects on the animal, she drew the line.

"Davis has no business showing that poor cat." Rachel opened and closed the cabinet a few times, testing the hinge. "He can't handle the stress, and she picks up on every bad vibe he puts out."

Sydney shook her head, wishing, not for the first time, that there was something more she could do. No laws had been broken, yet in her experience, the laws protecting animals actually did more to protect society's conscience. "I told him the same thing. As usual, he's ignoring my advice."

The door to the clinic opened. Sydney's heart skidded to a halt, then resumed at a maddening pace when Derek walked through the door, looking way too sexy for her peace of mind. Faded jeans rode low on his hips. A white polo shirt clung to his broad shoulders and emphasized his tanned biceps. His mouth drew her attention and held it, his lips tipped into a private smile just for her. Before she could stop herself, she answered his smile with one of her own.

"What are you doing here?" she asked, not bothering to question the unexplainable pleasure coursing through her. "Don't you have an afternoon lab?"

"Canceled." He stopped at the counter and propped his elbow, reminding her of a cowboy from one of those old Saturday-morning western movies sidling up to the bar and ordering a whiskey. "Wanna sneak away for a quick one?"

He might have been talking about lunch, but the low, sexy rumble of his voice, combined with the heated look in his eyes, said food was the last thing on his mind. Her pulse kicked into overdrive.

Rachel cleared her throat and stood, smothering a grin. "Hello, Dr. Buchanan."

Derek immediately straightened and looked a tad guilty. "Rachel. I...uh...didn't know you were here."

"So I gathered," she said in good humor, then pulled her purse from the bottom drawer of her desk. "I've got some errands to run. I'll lock up."

Sydney thought she was beyond blushing, until her cheeks heated. She could just imagine what her assistant was thinking.

"Sorry 'bout, that," Derek said once they were truly alone. The wicked gleam in his eyes and the oh-so-sexy grin made her doubt the sincerity of his apology.

"If you're interested in *lunch*," she told him, "I'll share my chicken sandwich and leftover seafood salad."

"It's a date," he said, then followed her down the corridor to her office.

Twenty minutes later, her suspicious nature flared to life. After the sexual innuendo and the I-want-you look in his eyes when he'd first come into the clinic, she fully expected him to launch into another matrimonial mission statement once they were alone. At the very least, perhaps a few exponents of his attributes as a family man or maybe another summation of the financial benefits of marriage. Instead, he told her about the university's decision to head up a new astrophysical research project. If it hadn't been for the slight tension in her tummy in response to his deep, resonant voice, or the fact that she couldn't stop thinking about kissing him, this could have been any other shared lunch.

By the time they cleared away the evidence of their impromptu picnic, the exhaustion she'd felt earlier returned. She shifted and rested her head against the arm of the sofa. No matter how rude, she yawned. "Sorry, I'm just a little tired."

"Sit up a minute." He moved so he was sitting directly beside her, then gently eased her down so her head rested against his thigh.

She gave him a skeptical look.

He gave her a tolerant one.

Surprisingly, the tension she'd been feeling since he'd arrived eased. She curled onto her side, suspecting that the soothing sound of his voice had lulled her into a state of relaxation. Surely it had nothing to do with the fact that his hand was alternately massaging her shoulder and smoothing her hair away from her face.

"Will you run the research?" she asked, stifling another yawn.

"We don't know who's heading up the research," he said after another lengthy and far too detailed explanation of the project, which she couldn't hope to understand. "I've got a good chance of being put on the team, but I'd wager Ken Eames will head it up. He did some pretty valuable research last year on a study of self-gravitating stellar systems."

"They'd be foolish not to give it to you," she

told him, and meant it. Derek was a scientist, and his love of astrophysics showed in everything he did, from teaching to working with various researchers, and even heading a few of his own projects. To her mind, he was brilliant, even if he didn't know which end of a screwdriver to use.

They fell silent, and she closed her heavy lids. "I shouldn't do this," she said quietly. "I've got a million things to do."

She felt the trail of his knuckles along her cheek. "Sh," he whispered. "Just rest."

As much as she wanted to follow his advice, she knew she shouldn't. "There's tons of work here, and at home," she murmured, in no hurry to move.

A final thought crossed her mind. Maybe it was the closeness to Derek that was keeping her resting her head against his thigh. She yawned, and the exhaustion finally claimed her.

DEREK KISSED HER AWAKE. When she moaned against his mouth and reached up to slip her arms around his neck, he shifted their bodies and deepened the kiss. She didn't protest, but arched her slender curves against him in an age-old invitation.

Heat flared, hardening him in a flash. What was it about this woman that made him want to forget his good intentions? While seducing Sydney was never far from his mind, his plan consisted of providing concrete evidence of why they should marry. He was supposed to show her how wonderful their life could be together. He couldn't recall any notation in the next phase of his experiment that included deep, tongue-tangling kisses.

Groaning deep in his throat, he followed her lead and welcomed the detour from his course of action. He nearly came out of his skin when she arched her back and rubbed her breasts provocatively against his chest. She was driving him insane and had his control precariously close to slipping. Her hands slid into his hair to hold him close. He had no intention of leaving any time soon.

He sensed her need, her heat, her desire, and as much as he wanted to satisfy the sensual demands of the woman torturing him with her sweet body and soul-reaching kisses, Rachel would be returning soon. He'd only meant to kiss her awake, not torment them both with something they had no time to finish.

Despite the desire coiled tightly inside him, he ended the kiss. He stared into her passion-softened green eyes and considered locking the door and putting out a Do Not Disturb for a Week sign.

"What are you doing to me?" Her slightly swollen lips curved into one of those secret feminine smiles that had the power to bring the males of the species to their knees.

"I know what I'd like to do," he told her, resisting the urge to show her exactly how much he wanted her.

She moaned softly, seductively, and pressed her body closer. "You make me want things, Derek. Things I have no business wanting."

He suspected her words were as close to the

truth as she was willing to admit. For the time being, her sweet confession had to be enough. There was little doubt in his mind that she loved him. The suspicion that there was something deeper preventing her from expressing the depth of her feelings nagged at him, but for now, he'd bide his time and wouldn't press for more than she was willing to give.

He eased off the sofa and away from the erotic promise in her eyes. "Stop looking at me like that," he teased. "Or I'll lock the door and ravish you."

Her answering chuckle was husky and filled with sin, doing nothing to ease his already uncomfortable jeans. Her eyes took a slow, studied tour of his body, stopping momentarily where the denim cupped his sex, then moved back to his face.

Her lips curved into a seductive grin.

His heart thundered in his chest.

He shoved his hands through his hair and pulled in a rough breath. "Don't start something we can't finish, Syd," he warned.

She moved off the sofa and strolled to the door. The lock snapped into place and his stomach bottomed out.

"You started it," she said, turning toward him. "Now finish it."

He backed up a step, then another, until his backside came in contact with her desk. As much as he wanted her, he wasn't about to risk her fiery retribution if her assistant should return and find them. "Wait a minute, what about…"

The words died on his lips when she spread her

hands over his chest then ran them down his torso to trace the waistband of his jeans. "You won't leave me like this." The confident, husky tone of her voice, combined with the red-hot need in her eyes, nearly killed the last shred of the nobility he was struggling to maintain.

Using her teeth, she nipped playfully at his throat. "You wouldn't leave me hot, would you?"

He tried to breathe, but his lungs felt ready to burst.

Her lips blazed a path of fire to his jaw. "Needy," she whispered.

He tried to swallow, but his mouth was as dry as dust.

She strained against him and gently nipped his ear. "And wet." Then she flicked the snap of his jeans.

Restraint and nobility fled. A groan rose from deep in his chest. He grabbed hold of her hips, pulling her tight against him. Her lips sought his in hot, openmouthed demand.

Sydney felt warm and dizzy as his hands skimmed her hips, inching the material of her sundress higher. She wanted him. It was that simple. She couldn't explain what made her forget that she was playing with fire, and she didn't think she wanted to know.

He broke the kiss suddenly, turning her around so her bottom was pressed against his straining arousal. She gripped the edge of the desk and held on tight when his mouth skimmed her ear, her neck and her jaw while his hand burned a path up her thigh to her hip. His fingers teased the elastic band on her panties, and her breath caught. She couldn't think straight. She ached with a fierce need to have him inside her.

His fingers edged beneath the elastic and traced the most intimate part of her. She shamelessly rubbed her bottom against his groin. A deep moan of pleasure escaped when he slid his finger deep inside her. Using his teeth and tongue, he grazed her jaw, her ear, her neck, adding to the flames licking through her. The intensity grew and peaked, then she whimpered, trembled, and fell apart in his arms.

He held her close, whispering sweet, gentle words in her ear while her ragged breathing slowed. She turned around and buried her face against his chest, luxuriating in the feel of his hands chasing down her spine in a soothing pattern.

Once her heart rate resumed a normal pace, she tipped her head back to look into his eyes. She saw the tenderness there and waited for the familiar cold chill to settle over her. Instead, she felt an answering warmth that had her wanting to snuggle against him. "That wasn't exactly what I had in mind."

"Do you hear me complaining?" He kissed her, long and slow, sweet and tender, stopping just before she followed through on the notion to close the clinic for the afternoon in pursuit of other, more sensual delights.

"I've got to go," he said. The reluctance in his voice pulled at a place deep inside her. Her heart? "I'll be back later."

Another gentle kiss, a gentle brush of his fingers across her cheek, and then he was gone.

Sydney pulled in a deep breath and let it out slowly. There was no way she could regret what had happened with Derek. But she was in trouble. Serious trouble.

Because she couldn't wait until later.

WHAT HAS he done now?

Sydney stood at the edge of the brick path leading to the cottage, staring in shocked disbelief at her front lawn. In the waning light of early dusk, the grass looked as if it had been neatly cut and edged. Then she peered closer and noticed patches of earth covered by wispy blades, like the head of a middle-aged man hoping to hide his receding hairline by combing what was left of his thinning hair over his baldness.

She sighed in exasperation, wishing she'd made the time to replace her old and tricky lawn mower. Every so often, adjustments were required or the mower cut too close, killing off sections of lawn. She couldn't be angry with Derek. His heart was in the right place, and she'd even made the same mistake herself a time or two when she forgot to check the settings on the cantankerous old machine.

She made a mental note to buy grass seed and a new mower.

She walked across the lawn to inspect the evergreen bushes beneath the picture window. He'd trimmed each hedge into a perfectly shaped box, and he'd even cleared the weeds and accumulated leaves from beneath the shrubs.

Okay, so he made a little mistake with the lawn, which really wasn't his fault. How could he know her mower needed repairing? A box or two of grass seed wasn't anything to get upset about. And besides, the hedges beneath the big picture window looked wonderful. Considering how *un*-handy Derek was, she did appreciate his thoughtfulness.

Until she slammed her toe against a misplaced brick on the path leading to the front door. She cried out. Pain shot through her foot. Tears sprang to her eyes. Someone turned on the porch light, which hadn't worked since she'd moved in, blinding her.

"Syd? What happened? Are you all right?"

She blinked against the harsh light, holding one hand in front of her face to protect her eyes, using the other to grip her throbbing foot. *Somebody save me from men with good intentions.*

"I'll be fine," she managed to reply through gritted teeth, surprised she didn't bite the poor guy's head off. Reminding herself he was only being helpful didn't stop the very unappreciative thoughts roaming through her mind.

She looked down at the brick path. Those nasty little blades of grass and weeds she'd been battling since moving into the cottage were no more. Testing the reliability of her foot, the brick beneath her wobbled. "Did you move the bricks?"

He smiled with pride, as if he'd just discovered the cure for the common cold. "I was worried about using chemicals. You know, the baby and all. So I moved the bricks, then laid down a roll of gardener's tarp. The guy in the lawn-and-garden center at the hardware store said you shouldn't have any more weed problems."

She stared at him, then down at the brick pathway, in disbelief. "You moved all of these bricks? By yourself?" The pathway had to be at least twenty-five feet long and three feet wide. "And put them back? Alone?"

He shrugged, as if he hadn't just accomplished the Herculean task without assistance.

What was one little stubbed toe compared to the joy he felt by doing her yard work? "Thank you, Derek." She limped toward him, trying not to wince with each painful step. "That was very sweet of you."

He took her hand, lacing their fingers together. "Wait until you see the inside."

She nearly groaned, but managed a weak smile instead and let him lead her into the house. To her surprise, the cottage practically glowed. The kitchen floor gleamed, the low cherry wood tables in the living room glistened. Even her prized crystal collection sparkled as it caught and reflected the soft lamplight.

A variety of scents assaulted her when she limped farther into the living room. Pine, lemon, lilac and—she sniffed the air. Egg foo young?

"Chan's?" she asked, hopeful. The small, hole-in-the-wall Chinese takeout near the Sound was one of their favorites, and she was deeply touched by his thoughtfulness.

Her heart beat just a little bit faster at the pleasure in his eyes. "I know how much you like it, and you were so tired earlier, I didn't think you'd feel like cooking."

She set her purse on the antique buffet she used as extra storage space. "I don't know what to say." Ever since she'd left her parents' home, she'd been taking care of herself. If anything needed doing, she took care of it, depending on no one.

He pulled her to him, slipping his arms around her. "You can thank me later."

Her pulse kicked into high gear. "Later?"

He brushed his lips gently against hers. "Later," he murmured, then captured her mouth in a breath-stealing kiss that curled her toes. Even the sore one.

He ended the kiss all too soon. "Hungry?"

Not for food, she thought, but kept the notion to herself. She nodded instead, and struggled to hide her disappointment when he dropped his arms to his side.

"The table's all set. I'll be right back."

Derek disappeared down the hall to wash up, so she slipped off her sandals and dropped them near the front door. She didn't know what to think anymore, and her confusion was mounting.

She wanted Derek. Wanted him with a ferocity that had taken her completely by surprise. He made no secret of the fact that he not only wanted her, but wanted to marry her. Only because he believed she was carrying his baby, she reminded herself. That was the reason for the change in their relationship. Or had they been heading in this very direction since her return from Kentucky?

Perhaps the old saying that men and women can't be friends was true. Eventually one of them ruins the friendship by wanting to have sex. Their friendship had certainly evolved from friends into something deeper. After the way she'd practically begged him to make love to her this afternoon, they definitely qualified as lovers.

But they weren't in love, she told herself. Derek wanted to marry her because she was pregnant, and for some reason she didn't care to analyze, he was convinced he was the father of her baby. Just because they'd become lovers, didn't mean she wanted to marry him, or even live with him. She had a child to think about now. What kind of example would she be setting for her child if she shacked up with some guy?

Not some guy.

Derek.

Her baby's father?

She shook her head and headed toward the kitchen. He was getting to her. He was gentle and sweet, thoughtful and caring, and her hormones were in an uproar and responding to every kind thing he said or did. There was no other logical explanation.

She was not in love with Derek.

"I'm not," she muttered to herself.

She stepped onto the cool kitchen tiles, but as she lifted her foot to take another step, her foot stuck and she had to peel it away from the tile. Frowning, she used her good toe and stepped on the tile again, then tried to lift her foot. "What on earth did he do now?"

"I mopped the floor for you."

She would have turned, but her feet were stuck, so she looked over her shoulder at him. "What did you use?"

His brows knit together in confusion. "That bottle of pine cleaner you had under the sink."

She leaned forward and reached for a chair. "Had? You used an entire bottle on this little floor?"

He came into the kitchen, the soles of his boots alternately squeaking and sticking with each step he took. He set the cartons of takeout on the table. "I put in what it said, but it never lathered up."

She managed to sit, then rested her feet against the pedestal of the table. "So you just kept pouring until you saw bubbles, is that it?"

He handed her the carton of egg foo young. "Shouldn't have done that, huh?"

How could she be angry with him when he looked so darned adorable? "No, Derek. You shouldn't have. You *really* shouldn't have."

She added floor stripper to her mental shopping list, thankful he'd only mopped the kitchen and not the hardwood floors she'd worked so hard to restore.

She slid the crystal bowl of fresh pansies aside and reached for the fried rice.

Her hand stilled. She looked at the crystal bowl, and her heart sank. "Are these from my garden?" she asked.

"I'm sorry, Syd," he said, his voice filled with contrition. "The mower got away from me."

Dread filled her. When she'd first moved into the cottage, the property had been a disaster. The cottage had been used for storage, and the yards hadn't been tended to in years. She'd spent nearly as many hours working in the yard as she did in the clinic. "Got away from you how?"

He set his fork on the edge of his plate and looked at her, his gaze filled with guilt. "I let it sit for a minute while I moved the hose out of the way. I thought it would idle."

"It didn't."

"No," he said, and shook his head. "It moved."

"Moved? Moved how far?"

"It took off."

"Took off?"

"Uh-huh."

"Through my flower bed?"

"Uh-huh."

"How bad is it?"

"Well, you might want to consider relandscaping."

Accidents happened, she told herself. They just happened more often to Derek when he was trying to play…husband? Is that what this was all about? she wondered. All the work he'd done in the yard, all the cleaning and dusting and mopping almost made sense, if that was indeed his ulterior motive. And she had a bad feeling that it was. "Derek, what else did you do today?"

He smiled. "Laundry."

Her heart sank. "Oh, sweet heaven."

"Hey, I can handle the laundry."

"Did you turn my lab coats pink?"

"No," he said, looking a bit put out by her lack of faith.

"You separated colors from the whites?"

"And dark colors from the lighter ones," he said, sounding miffed.

Fear, and not wanting to further injure his

pride, kept her from asking if he'd remembered to use cold water for the colors. She took the egg roll he offered, deciding she didn't want to know. Sometimes, ignorance *was* bliss.

7

THE NEW MOON glowed like a silver beacon in the night sky, while the serenade of crickets and a light breeze from the Sound created the perfect accompaniment for a romantic evening. Too bad Syd wasn't into romance, Derek thought looking for a particular star. But he wasn't about to complain since he couldn't have asked for a more perfect setting to initiate the next phase of his experiment.

"Ah, there it is." He leaned close to Sydney and pointed toward the constellation, torturing himself as he breathed in her scent. With very little coaxing, he'd convinced her to join him under the guise of a little stargazing while he attempted to discover the cause for her objections to marriage. "Ursa Major."

She tipped her head back and looked up at the stars. He admired the slender column of her throat. Only every ounce of willpower he possessed kept him from ducking his head to tease the sensitive spot behind her ear that would have her slipping her arms around his neck and arching against him. Although altering his testable theory midstream strained his patience and would no doubt increase his level of sexual frustration to the point of pain, he'd made a decision and planned to follow through. No more sex. The plan might kill him, but he wasn't going to make love to her again until she agreed to a commitment, one sanctified by a priest. Of course, that didn't mean he wouldn't use every weapon in his arsenal to stir her senses and make her see he was dead serious...about them.

"It's the Big Dipper," she said, and shrugged.

Not about to be put off by her less than enthusiastic response, he said, "It's also called the Great Bear by some of the North American tribes—the Iroquois, I think. It's also the third largest constellation."

"That's very interesting, Derek."

She didn't sound interested. She sounded bored. Didn't all women find the idea of Indian lore romantic? "It's also believed to be the Greek nymph Callisto."

She glanced at him, a slight frown marring her brow. "Who?"

"Callisto." He laid his arm on the back of the porch swing. His fingers intentionally brushed her neck and his mouth quirked when she visibly shivered. "In Greek mythology, she was the daughter of King Lycaon, and chosen to be one of Artemis's companions."

"Wasn't Artemis Apollo's sister?" She looked at him again. Her luminous green eyes held questions, but not the one she'd just asked. Oh no, she was curious, wondering if he was going to finish what they'd started earlier this afternoon.

He nodded, and loosened the clip binding her rich, sable waves. "Artemis was the patroness of childbirth and the protector of babies and animals," he told her, sifting his fingers through the silken strands. "The one thing she prized above all else was her chastity. She even asked Zeus for eternal virginity."

The grin canting her lips was more than wicked, it was filled with erotic promise that had him doubting his ability to adhere to his new no-sex-without-commitment rule. "How sad," she whispered. "She didn't know what she was missing."

He shifted in his seat, cursing his rotten timing. He cleared his throat and concentrated on the Greek myth, instead of the instant heat glowing in her gaze. "All of the nymphs Artemis surrounded herself with reflected her own vows of chastity, but she also demanded absolute fidelity from them."

Sydney's gaze traveled over his face and settled on his mouth. Using her tongue, she moistened her bottom lip, and he nearly groaned. The urge to capture her sweet mouth beneath his own, to delve inside and taste all of her secrets, was strong.

"Except Zeus had his own ideas," he said instead, tearing his gaze from hers. "And a bad habit of seducing young maidens, pretty little Callisto included. She became pregnant with Zeus's child, and when Artemis heard about it, she pitched a fit and took her revenge. Since she loved to hunt, she decided to extract her vengeance by turning Callisto into a bear. Her plan was to have the young maiden hunted down and killed."

Surprise momentarily flashed in Sydney's eyes. "Oh, how horrible!"

His fingers moved from her hair to gently massage the back of her neck. "Zeus took pity, and sent Callisto to the heavens."

"The bear," she said, letting her head fall slightly forward to give him better access. A soft moan escaped. "Hmm, that feels wonderful."

He could think of a few dozen other things that would have her soft little moan turning into a cry of satisfaction.

She lifted her feet onto the bench of the swing and rested her back against him. Without hesitation, he slipped his arm around her, drawing lazy patterns over the soft-as-silk skin on her shoulder. She snuggled closer.

Sydney was an impossible mixture of contradictions, and she was driving him crazy. She shifted gears faster than a Ferrari, and he was having one hell of a time keeping up with her. One minute bright-yellow warning signs were posted all around her, keeping away trespassers, and the next she was curled against him, stirring his most natural and basic instincts. Telling himself that in time he'd find a way around all those No Trespassing signs to the heart of the woman he loved offered little comfort. He was starting to feel as if he were spinning his wheels and getting nowhere fast.

She laid her head against his shoulder to look up at the star-filled sky. "Zeus was a bit of a scoundrel, wasn't he?"

He chuckled. "Unlike Zeus, I'm a one-woman man."

She stiffened, the tension in her body filling him with caution. Instinct told him he'd hit a nerve.

Dammit, he knew she loved him. He felt it in her response to his lovemaking when she opened her soul to him. He saw the emotion in her luminous eyes when she looked at him. He'd seen pleasure light up her face when he'd surprised her by coming to the clinic that afternoon. Something was keeping her from committing to him, and he was determined to find out what it was. He threw caution aside.

"What happened to you, Syd? Your parents had a great marriage, so I just don't get it. Did someone forget to tell you about fairy tales and happily-ever-after when you were a little girl?"

She swung her feet to the ground and stood. "Happily-ever-after *is* a fairy tale," she said with a touch of steel in her voice. "It's getting late. You'd better leave."

She walked into the house, leaving him frustrated and confused. He wasn't about to be dismissed so easily. He'd struck a nerve, and had no intention of allowing her to retreat inside herself. Not tonight. Tonight he was going to find out why she kept stonewalling him, patience be damned.

He found her in the living room, sitting on the far corner of the floral sofa, her feet curled beneath her. She looked small and alone, but he expected her spirit to return once he pushed her into expressing those emotions she kept buried.

He hitched his thumbs into the front pockets of

his jeans. "You're wrong, Syd," he told her gently. "If two people love each other—"

"Love?" She gave a caustic little laugh that had him frowning. "It doesn't exist."

He circled the sofa and crouched in front of her, resting his hand on her knee. "How do you know that until you give it a try?"

Sydney stared down at Derek. Tenderness, and that other emotion she refused to believe in, glowed in his eyes and sent a shiver of fear racing down her spine. "You're fooling yourself," she said, and stood. She needed space. She needed him to drop this ridiculous tangent and just be her friend.

"No, Syd." He looked up at her, and she felt an achy emptiness inside her. "Not about us, I'm not. You love me, but you're afraid."

Her breath caught and lodged in her throat. She did not love him. She couldn't. She cared for him, but love? Never again would she subject herself to such foolishness in a game with rules she didn't understand. The scars she bore from the last round marked her with a constant reminder of what could happen if she let down her guard, and God forbid, dared to trust again.

"Love is a nonexistent emotion created by greeting card companies and florists to pad their balance sheets," she told him with more defensive heat than she'd intended. "You're a scientist, for crying out loud. You of all people should know better than to believe in the existence of something that can't be proven."

He stood and faced her, frustration filling his

eyes. "Just because love isn't empirically testable doesn't mean it's nonexistent."

Her heartbeat pounded like thunder. Dread snaked through her. "This isn't about love," she managed to reply around the growing pressure in her throat. "You've convinced yourself you're the father of my baby. It's just some male, macho thing that you need to get over."

Something dark and dangerous flickered in his narrowed gaze, as if she'd pushed him too far. "You don't know that I'm not the father." A hardness crept into his voice that should have warned her to put an end to the conversation.

She ignored the warning. "And you don't know that you are," she shot back in frustration. "We've had this argument before. You know how I feel."

"I know you're being stubborn, and for some reason I can't understand, you're unwilling to even consider what could be the truth."

She stared at him in utter astonishment. There was no truth. There was no love. It didn't exist. Why couldn't he see that? "Because I don't want to get married, to you or anyone, does not make me stubborn."

He advanced toward her, but she held her ground. "It makes me smarter than the rest of you fools running around thinking that love is the answer for—"

"For what, Syd?" he asked, settling his hands on her shoulders. She wished she'd changed into something with more material, then she wouldn't feel the raspy warmth of his hands on her bare skin, or the answering tingle in the pit of her stomach.

"For the warmth you feel whenever you see me? For the pleasure that runs through you whenever I touch you?" He slid his hands over her shoulders, down her arms and up again to her throat. His thumbs teased the underside of her jaw, forcing her to look into his bluer than sin eyes, forcing her to see the emotion that had the power to make her doubt her choices, if she let it.

"For the way you lie awake at night and think about me inside you?"

The husky purr of his quiet voice had erotic images flashing through her mind. Deep in her stomach, the tingles ignited. "That's lust," she said in a shaky voice.

"Baby, it's a whole lot more than lust, and you know it. But you're so busy running scared, you can't see what's right in front of you." The intensity of the shrewd, assessing glint in his eyes had her nearly believing him.

An awful pressure clamped her chest. "No," she said, stepping away from him, away from the heat, away from the confusion. Away from the truth? "We're friends. That's all we can ever be."

"We're a helluva lot more than friends," he said, planting his hands on his hips.

He was right. As much as she feared what that admission could cost her emotionally, they'd crossed the line from friendship to lovers, and there was no going back. But they couldn't go forward, either, or follow the natural progression into deeper, more emotional territory. Not if there was even the slightest chance he wasn't the father of her baby. She wouldn't subject her child to the pain of having someone he loved and trusted reject him.

"Derek, please. I don't want—"

"No, Syd. I'm not going to let you run away from the truth this time. I know you love me."

She shook her head, but it didn't remove the truth banked in his eyes, or the fear clawing at her insides that he could be right. "No!"

"You do, but you're afraid. Why?"

She wrapped her arms around her middle and fought a losing battle with the moisture clouding her gaze. "I'm not afraid of you or anyone," she said, but the force of her words lost their impact because of the waver in her voice.

His reply was blunt and mildly profane. "Try again," he said harshly. "What happened to you in Kentucky?"

He knew. Somehow he knew that she'd been a fool, that she'd once believed in love, in happily-ever-after and all the joy of finding that one special person to share her life with. But how could he? She'd never told a soul what Nicholas had done to her, or worse, the pain and heartache an innocent child suffered because of one man's resentment. Not even Rachel knew about Nicholas, and she probably classified as her closest female friend.

"I… Nothing happened. It's none of your business."

He closed the space between them, cupping her face in his warm palms. "What did he do to you, Syd?" he asked with more gentleness, tearing her already tattered heart.

"He's in the past. It's over." She tried to look away, but he nudged her chin with his thumb so she had no choice but to look into his eyes.

"He's right here between us," he said quietly, "because you won't let him go."

He was wrong, but that didn't stop a deep chill from settling around her. He was wrong. He had to be. "I thought you were a scientist." She pulled away from him and moved to the other side of the room. "Since when did you start practicing psychoanalysis?"

He stayed cool, unruffled, despite her patronizing tone. "I don't need a degree in psych to know that whatever number this guy pulled on you, it's keeping you from being happy."

She crossed her arms over her chest and glared at him. "Well you're wrong, Sigmund Freud. I'm plenty happy. I have a successful business, a home. I have everything I could possibly need to be happy."

An undercurrent of sadness crept into his eyes. It kept her rooted to the spot as he slowly approached. "Material possessions aren't the same as sharing your life with someone."

She defiantly lifted her chin. "I don't need anyone. I depend on no one but myself."

He lifted his hand and gently ran his knuckles down her cheek. "That's where you're wrong, sweetheart," he said quietly. "Because everyone needs someone at some point in their lives."

She looked away, and he dropped his hand to his side. "Even you," he added, before striding to the door.

The snap of the latch when he closed the door

behind him reverberated through her. She had the fleeting thought that she'd seen the last of him, but she quickly squelched the panic threatening to engulf her.

"You're wrong," she whispered to the quiet room, thankful Derek couldn't hear the lack of conviction in her tear-strained voice.

SYDNEY TOSSED aside the bed covers. Since giving the puppies their midnight feeding, she'd abandoned all hope of falling asleep. For the past two hours, she'd tossed and turned, and now she couldn't stand another minute of lying in bed staring at the ceiling. Thinking about Derek. Wanting him. Dammit, needing him.

Pulling her cotton robe off the chair, she shrugged into it as she left the bedroom and made her way through the darkened cottage to the kitchen. Maybe a cup of tea would soothe her rattled nerves, but she wasn't holding out much hope.

She didn't bother flipping on the overhead light as she crossed the sticky floor in her bare feet, but snapped the switch for the light above the stove, instead. After filling the kettle and setting it to heat, she opened the back door and slipped outside into the sultry warmth of the night.

She curled her toes over the smooth edge of cobblestone and peered up at the sky filled with stars. Did Derek ever see them as millions of twinkling diamonds scattered across endless yards of black satin, or were they just subjects to be studied and analyzed with a telescope? She spotted the Big Dipper, or Callisto the nymph turned bear, wondering what had gone wrong tonight.

Unless she was willing to call herself a liar, she couldn't deny the charged sexual energy that sparked whenever they were together any more than she could continue to ignore that the feelings Derek evoked went deeper than friendship. Something had happened that went beyond their making love and possibly creating a child together. Something she feared, yet felt herself beginning to crave against her will. She didn't have a clue how to prevent being pulled deeper and deeper into the whirlwind of emotions she was afraid to name, and didn't know whether or not to trust.

She could accept that they'd become lovers. The physical aspect of their relationship was easy. It was his demands for more on an emotional level that had her...running scared?

No, she told herself. Her emotions were on the surface because of the hormonal changes in her body due to the pregnancy, and that was all, she told herself firmly. Other than much needed nap time that had started to plague her the past few days, emotional upheaval and exhaustion were her only symptoms thus far, along with a burning need to be with Derek in the most intimate way possible. She'd have to check a recent book on pregnancy to see if heightened sexual awareness was also a symptom of pregnancy.

The shrill whistle of the teakettle shook her out of her thoughts, and she strolled back into the cottage. Since sleep was out of the question for the time being, she carried her tea into the living room and decided to fold the laundry Derek had so thoughtfully done for her.

She found the wicker basket atop the dryer with a few linens folded neatly inside, then opened the dryer and tossed the clothes into the basket. With the basket tucked under her arm, she walked back to the living room, turned on the lamp, then the television. After cruising through the late-night talk shows and infomercials, she finally found an old Clark Gable and Claudette Colbert movie in black and white she'd seen dozens of times and always enjoyed.

What more could a woman want?

She ignored the answer that instantly popped into her head, and settled back on the sofa, determined not to think about her argument with Derek.

Until she reached into the basket and pulled out what had once been an expensive silk blouse reserved for dry cleaning only. She stared in disbelief at the pale-mint-green blouse she always wore with her favorite cream slacks. It looked as if it would fit Rachel's eight-year-old daughter!

"Oh, no," she whined, realizing Derek had washed the stack of clothes she'd set aside for the dry cleaner.

Her heart sank when she picked up her favorite off-white lamb's wool sweater, which now resembled something upscale and trendy for a child's fashion-model doll. Even though the sweater had been on sale when she'd bought it, it had still come with a ridiculously high price tag. She rarely spent much money on clothes, preferring to spend her time in surgeon's scrubs or a lab coat tossed over a T-shirt and jeans, but occasionally she treated herself to something decadent and expensive.

His heart was in the right place.

"The man's impossible!" she rallied against her conscience. "Of all the…"

But he meant well.

With a disgusted sigh, she tossed Barbie's new lamb's wool sweater back into the basket. What could she do? Nothing that wouldn't hurt Derek's feelings or wound that oversize male ego of his. And she'd never consciously hurt him.

He'd never hurt you, either.

She scowled at her conscience, reached for her tea and stared at the television screen as Gable slung a thick blanket over a makeshift clothesline in an attempt to divide the single room he was to share with Claudette for the night. A true hero, she thought, protecting his lady's honor.

Was that what Derek was trying to do? she wondered. Was he trying to protect her honor by offering to marry her? Or did his backhanded, and sometimes insulting, proposals stem from something much more basic and elemental—his belief in that elusive emotion he kept referring to, the one she refused to acknowledge existed.

She had no easy answers. In fact, she was becoming more confused with each passing day. How could she want someone physically as much as she wanted Derek, yet be afraid of him at the same time? She didn't fear him in the classic sense, but she feared the way he made her feel, the way he made her forget her staunch arguments, the way he made her want things better left alone.

She feared the way he touched her heart, a heart she'd been convinced lay cold in her chest. And the way she thought about him at odd times throughout the day, during the most mundane tasks. And the way her pulse would beat just a little faster whenever she answered the phone and heard his voice on the other end.

But more than anything, she feared that he'd touched her soul...and she may never be the same again.

THE WOLF DEN was quiet for a Thursday night. Since the end of the term, a large portion of the academic population had fled Seattle for other parts of the country. His summer class schedule was late, and Derek found himself with far too much time on his hands.

He hadn't seen or heard from Sydney since their argument Monday night, and considering his mood the past three days, that was probably for the best. He'd never known a more stubborn woman, or a woman who could twist him up in knots so tight he couldn't think straight.

"Twice in the same week? Must be a woman."

Derek looked up from the beer he'd been nursing for the past hour into Leonard's scruffy face. "What makes you say that?"

Leonard propped his elbow against the bar. "You've got the look, Professor."

Derek wasn't in the mood for advice for the lovelorn, especially from the burly, Harley-loving philosopher, but it didn't look as if ol' Lenny was in a hurry to part company, especially when he signaled the waitress for a couple of beers.

"What look is that?" Derek asked.

Leonard smiled, showing off a gold-framed tooth. "That she's-breakin'-my-heart look. You hang around this place as much as I do, and you see it enough to know the signs."

"She's not breaking my heart," Derek said, then tipped back the bottle to drain the last of the now warm beer.

Leonard nodded his thanks to the waitress, then slid another cold one in front of Derek. "Ah, then it must have been a mutual, loving confrontation. A good, healthy part of any relationship."

Derek gripped the cold amber bottle in his hands, tracing the rivulets of condensation with his thumb. "Come again?"

"You had a fight and she threw you out," Leonard said, pulling a pack of cigarettes from the pocket of his black T-shirt.

"Not exactly," Derek said after some thought. He'd walked out, and had planned to wait for her to come to the realization that he was right, but after three days, he was considering admitting defeat. Since every single one of his theories had failed, he was out of options. Hell, he'd even made it clear that he loved her, and that hadn't come close to swaying her. Instead, he'd handed her the remaining bricks she needed to close herself off from him completely.

"She's just too damned stubborn for her own good and can't see what's right in front of her," Derek muttered.

Leonard nodded sympathetically. "Relationships are hard work, Professor. According to Peck, anyway."

Derek was vaguely familiar with the work of Scott Peck, a modern day psychiatrist and philosopher. "There's my problem, Lenny. I want a relationship. She claims she doesn't."

"But you think she does."

"I know she does," he said vehemently. She wanted him, physically and emotionally. He just had to find a way to convince her she could trust him.

"You do know that for a relationship to achieve its natural satisfying conclusion, it must be grounded in commitment."

Derek raked his hand through his hair in frustration. "I know that. But how do I convince her?"

Leonard lit the cigarette he shook from the pack and inhaled deeply. "You have to understand why she fears commitment," he said after a moment.

"I've tried."

"Have you asked her about it?"

Derek thought about their argument. Maybe he needed to be more insistent with her, force her to tell him what happened to her in Kentucky. And let her know, in no uncertain terms, exactly what he wanted from her. The truth. *And* a commitment.

"If you really love her," Leonard said, "it'll be evident through your actions, and she'll see it— eventually."

"I've tried just about everything I can think of, and nothing seems to work." He explained his theories and how each one of them failed to generate the desired results.

By the time Derek finished his diatribe, Leonard was shaking his head in dismay. The burly bouncer laughed, a huge gusty sound that rang in Derek's ears and drew the waitress's attention.

"Professor," Leonard said, "you've got a lot to learn about women. They want romance."

"Who wants romance?" the waitress asked as she cleared away an empty bowl of popcorn.

"The professor's woman," Leonard said in spite of Derek's warning look.

The waitress slapped a damp towel on the bar in front of them. "You mean a flowers-and-candy kind of romance?"

At Lenny's nod, the waitress agreed.

"Uh-uh," Derek disagreed. "No way. Not her."

The waitress gave him a stern look. "Why not?" she asked, as if he'd just offended the entire feminine class. "She's a woman, isn't she? She wants to feel special."

"I've jumped through enough hoops trying to get her to see how I feel about her." His back still ached from all the yard and household chores he'd done for her. If he never looked at another brick in his life, it'd be too soon. And he'd practically ruined a perfectly good pair of boots trying to remove that blasted peach paint from the soles. He was starting to feel as if he was in the middle of a damned dog-and-pony show performing tricks for a maniacal ringmaster.

"Have you told her?" the waitress asked.

"Hell, yes." He picked up the bottle and

pointed it at the waitress. "And it hasn't made a dent in that armor of hers."

Leonard laid a beefy hand on Derek's shoulder in a gesture he thought might be comforting. "Everyone has a chink in their armor, Professor. You just need to find hers."

"Try a little romance," the waitress added before moving down the bar.

"She's right," Leonard confirmed. "At this point, what have you got to lose?"

Nothing, Derek thought. *And everything.*

8

AFTER ANOTHER hectic day, Sydney unwound by taking her time to enjoy the antics of the litter of puppies. At four weeks old, they were eating solid food and raising a ruckus in the four-foot-square whelping box. Personalities had begun to develop, and a chubby, solid black male had established himself as the leader of the pack, until the little brindle female that Rachel favored noticed him expressing his dominance and quickly set proper order among the pack again.

"She's my kind of woman," Rachel said with a laugh when the female started to bark orders at the others.

"You should bring your daughters over to play with them." Sydney picked up the male and held him close, smiling when he nuzzled her neck. "They're old enough now and the socialization will be good for them."

Rachel gave her a skeptical look. "You trying to saddle me with a puppy, Sydney? Because that's a surefire way of making certain I take at least one."

Sydney smiled at her assistant. "I'd never do anything quite so underhanded. But maybe you should bring Steve along, too."

Rachel reached into the whelping box and

scooped the brindle into her arms. "It's not his decision, because yours truly will be the one taking care of her."

"Have you picked out a name?" Sydney asked, casting a sly glance at her assistant.

Rachel held the pup up to eye level. "She looks like an Alana, don't you think?" Both women laughed.

Rachel lowered the pup and cuddled her against her chest, peering at Sydney over the pup's head. "So, what's up with you and Dr. Buchanan? I haven't seen him around lately."

Sydney sighed and set the pup back in the box with his litter mates, not quite knowing how to answer. She hadn't heard a word from Derek since their argument two weeks ago. At first she'd thought she missed the friendship and companionship they'd always shared, but she couldn't keep lying to herself. She missed *him*, the way a woman misses that one special man in her life. She missed his warmth, his tenderness, his caring. She missed his well-intentioned but hapless attempts to convince her to marry him. As much as she hated to admit it, she longed to hear the sound of his voice, his laughter, and see that I-want-you look in his deep blue eyes. Her body craved his, along with the thrum of anticipation whenever he kissed her, and how she melted just a little every time he touched her and held her in his arms.

They were standing on opposite sides of a metaphorical canyon with neither one willing to take those first steps that would bring them together in the middle. He wanted marriage and would accept no less. She couldn't marry him, not if there was even the slightest chance that Derek wasn't the father.

"We had a disagreement," she finally said, giving in to the unaccustomed need to talk to someone.

Rachel nodded slowly. "A big disagreement?"

Sydney sighed again. "Unfortunately, yes. He said I was stubborn."

"You? Stubborn?" Rachel said in mock surprise.

Sydney frowned at her assistant. "I have my reasons," she muttered. Reasons she didn't think she could share with Derek. But he was wrong. She wasn't keeping the memory of Nicholas between them, only the valuable lesson she'd learned and a sense of guilt, no matter how misplaced. And maybe a teeny bit of stubbornness, too.

Rachel set the pup back in with the others and stood. "Reasons good enough to keep you away from the man you're in love with?" she asked in that calm, soothing way she had of making people open up to her. Sydney had seen her use that skill with her daughters, customers, even the UPS delivery guy, and instantly became suspicious.

"I'm *not* in love with him," she said in a haughty tone.

"No, of course, you're not," Rachel replied in an offhand manner, her attention riveted on smoothing nonexistent wrinkles in her slacks.

Sydney narrowed her gaze. She wasn't falling for Rachel's talk-show-confessional tone. "I'm not, Rach."

Her assistant shrugged. "I know. That's what you said."

"I don't believe in love," she added defensively.

Rachel straightened and gave her a level stare. "You're afraid of getting hurt, and I can understand that, but think about what you're missing if you let him slip away. Do you really want to spend the rest of your life wondering 'what if?'"

Sydney frowned. *What if?* What if she opened her heart and he trampled it? What if she wasn't carrying his baby? What if she did agree to marry him and he ended up resenting her, or worse, her child, when at some point they discovered the baby wasn't his?

What if he is the father? her conscience taunted.

Then she'd be denying her child the love and guidance of a very caring man.

Rachel ended their conversation by saying she needed to run her daughters to softball practice. By the time Sydney took care of the golden retriever she was boarding, made sure the puppies were settled for the night and locked up the clinic, she still hadn't made a decision. She crossed the gravel parking lot to the darkened cottage, dreading the thought of spending another night alone.

Not alone, she amended. Another night without Derek.

She walked along the brick path, a few of the bricks wobbling beneath her feet, and a reluctant grin tugged her lips. Maybe she should just pick up the phone and call him. At least he couldn't keep calling her stubborn if she made the first attempt to mend the rift between them.

As she neared the porch, her eyes widened in surprise. Propped near the front door sat a vase filled with deep-red roses. She hurried up the steps and breathed in the rich, heady fragrance. She didn't need to look at the card to know they were from Derek, but her heart soared just the same when she spied his bold script on the small white envelope.

She carefully pulled the envelope from the plastic holder and opened the card which read: "Dinner at 8:00? I'll pick you up."

Oh, he is a slick one, she thought. Whether or not she planned to accept his invitation, she'd have to see him, but she figured he was banking on her being unable to resist such a romantic invitation.

And he was right!

She only had an hour before Derek arrived, so she carried the vase into the cottage and set the roses on the antique buffet before heading into the bedroom to shower and change. She felt silly and giddy and warm all over. She wanted him, but that didn't mean she had to marry him. Tonight she'd let him know exactly what she wanted—a no-strings affair.

Despite all her warnings that she could very well be heading straight into another mistake, for better or worse, she couldn't wait to see him again.

It was that simple.

And that complicated.

THERE WAS MORE to this romantic stuff than Derek anticipated.

The thought of yet another screwup left a bad taste in his mouth, so like any good scientist, he'd conducted extensive research on the subject. After nearly two weeks of poring over the mountain of books he'd checked out of the university library, he'd come to one solid conclusion—he'd definitely taken the wrong approach in convincing Sydney they were made for each other.

Volume after volume had covered his desk, his kitchen table and nightstand as he researched the various forms of romance. He probably now knew more about the art of love than Casanova or Don Juan, and had formed a solid plan that didn't include hefting a few hundred pounds of brick, dusting and scrubbing, or folding sheets and towels. If he wanted to make a lasting impression and capture the heart of the woman he loved, flowers, candlelight dinners, jewelry, poetry and a little mystery had a better chance of success than his charts, graphs and logic.

At precisely 8:00 p.m., he eased his Explorer next to her Jeep and killed the engine. So far, all his research had gone according to plan. He'd confirmed the delivery of the flowers, and as one volume dictated, he'd kept the twelfth rose to present to her when he picked her up for the romantic dinner at a seafood restaurant overlooking the Sound. He slid from the vehicle and gave the pocket of his sport coat a pat, reassuring himself he hadn't forgotten the small white box containing the prerequisite gift of jewelry. He'd scratched the poetry idea. A man had to draw the line somewhere, especially since the only word he could think of that rhymed with Sydney was kidney.

With one hand holding the rose behind his back, he rang the bell. Every second he waited, his nervousness mounted, but when she finally eased the door open, tension fled and other more virulent emotions jockeyed for position.

Lust took the lead.

She was simply...beautiful, he thought. Her thick sable waves were pinned up by dozens of tiny emerald-tipped pins that matched her eyes. A few strands remained free down the curve of her nape. Only a pair of rhinestone-and-emerald earrings interrupted all that smooth-as-silk skin. His gaze traveled the length of her, from the thin straps holding the black sheath dress, to black silk stockings covering her shapely legs, then back up to where she held a single rose, twirling the soft petals so they brushed the scooped neckline of her dress and teased the gentle swell of her breasts.

His mouth went dry.

"Wow, you look great," he said, once he rediscovered the ability to form a declarative sentence.

"Thank you, Derek. Would you like to come in?"

Was it his overactive imagination, or had her voice really gone all sultry and sinful on him? *Imagination*, he decided firmly. Otherwise, all those wonderfully erotic thoughts threatening to overload his neurotransmitters would have him forgetting all about his cardinal rule.

No commitment—no sex.

And a stupid rule at that, he thought, his libido climbing quickly.

"We should be going," he said. "We have a reservation."

She reached over to take something off the buffet, drawing his attention to the rising hemline of her dress, which barely reached midthigh.

He swallowed.

Hard.

Damn!

They hadn't even made it out the door and already his plan of seducing her senses was backfiring on him. If she kept looking at him with those swallow-him-alive eyes, he just might have to break his rule....

She stepped through the door and stopped in front of him. Her tongue slicked over her bottom lip, and all he could think about was all her hot, sweet flavors just waiting to be savored.

"Thank you for the roses," she said, still using that sultry-soft voice that nearly had his determination to keep his hands to himself crumbling to dust.

"It was my pleasure."

Roses! Cripes, he almost forgot.

His hand snaked out, and he offered her the rose the way a little kid would share all the cool rocks and string he'd collected in his pockets.

She lifted the flower from his palm. Briefly closing her eyes, she breathed in its fragrance. When her lashes lifted, he stared into her eyes and his breath lodged firmly in his throat. If he'd known roses would put that hunger in her radiant green gaze, he'd have bought her an entire garden of them.

Placing his hand on the small of her back, he led her to the Explorer, then held the door for her while she climbed inside the truck. The hem of that dress inched upward again, giving him a generous glimpse of lace-topped stockings. His heartbeat thudded in his chest. He didn't know how much more of this he could take, but man, oh man, what a way to go.

Get a grip, buddy boy. You've got a long night ahead of you. A very long night.

SYDNEY TOYED with her Caesar salad, and cast another surreptitious glance at Derek in the soft, golden glow of the tapered candles. He talked about the new research project, and while she was thrilled with the boost that heading the project was giving to his career, she couldn't help be curious about what he was up to this time. He acted as if nothing had happened, as if they'd never argued and as if their not seeing each other during the past two weeks was nothing out of the ordinary.

But that wasn't her only concern.

She knew he'd been affected by her blatant siren song when she'd met him at the door, so his good-buddy-good-pal routine now stung her feminine pride. Since they'd arrived at the elegant, upscale restaurant, she hadn't caught so much as a glimmer of interest, sexual or otherwise.

She set her fork aside and reached for the crystal water glass. He concentrated on adding a hefty dose of pepper to his salad.

"Anyway," he said, exchanging pepper for salt, "the X-ray luminosity can't be explained by starbursts."

"Derek?"

"But, since the apparent optical counterpart shows the required characteristics of a narrow line X-ray galaxy with a red-shift of 0.107—"

"Derek?"

"—and since the H_beta luminosity is—"

"Derek!"

Startled, he looked up from his salad. "Sorry," he said after a moment's hesitation. An adorable, sheepish grin tugged at his lips. "I was getting too technical again, wasn't I?"

"To say the least," she said wryly, setting her glass aside. The gold bangle bracelet he'd given her earlier, glinted in the candlelight. "Thank you again." She smoothed her fingers over the classic gold circle. "This was very unexpected, and much appreciated."

"I'm glad you like it," he said quietly, setting the salt shaker on the white linen tablecloth. He scooted closer in the booth and reached for her hand. Bringing her fingers to his lips, he lightly brushed his mouth across her knuckles, sending a delightful shiver racing down her spine. "Too bad it's not small enough to fit on your finger."

She pulled her hand free, wishing just for once they could get through an evening without a discussion of marriage. Why couldn't he just accept the fact that while she had no qualms about being lovers, matrimony was a badge she had no intention of earning. "Derek, I don't—"

He lifted his hand to stop her denial. "We should talk."

Uh-oh. "About?"

"You. Me. And whatever happened to you in Kentucky."

She sighed. She had to tell him, otherwise he'd continue to try to badger her into marrying him. But the fear that he'd judge her nearly had her changing the subject.

"Trust me, Syd."

She briefly closed her eyes. He had no clue what he was asking. Trust. She'd given it once, along with her heart, and both had been carelessly trampled in an emotional stampede she'd been powerless to prevent.

She lifted her lashes and looked at him. His tone may have been coaxing and filled with patience, but there was a glint of hardness in his eyes that made her wonder if he wasn't issuing a gently cloaked demand. "It's not that easy."

He slipped his hand over hers, entwining their fingers together. "You'd be surprised how easy it really is...if you're willing to try."

If you're willing to open your heart, was the look she detected in his eyes.

With her free hand, she reached for her glass and took a sip of water to ease the dry achiness of her throat. "I don't know where to start."

His thumb rubbed lightly over hers. "Try the beginning," he suggested. "How did you meet him?"

She waited for the pain of betrayal to grip her,

and was surprised when all she felt was the sense of misplaced guilt that always plagued her whenever she thought about Nicholas. Maybe she hadn't loved him as much as she'd believed. Maybe she'd been in love with the idea of what she and Nicholas could have accomplished together, of the great team they could have made professionally, rather than with the man himself. She sighed, knowing she'd never have the answers. But perhaps they weren't as important as she'd once thought. Perhaps Derek had been correct. Nicholas was a part of her past, and while she'd never forget the betrayal, until she was willing to let go, her past would always be between them.

She pulled in a deep breath to shore up her courage. "Nicholas Adams was a horse trainer," she began slowly, turning her gaze to the flickering taper. "One of the best racing trainers in the country. He worked with some of the top breeders in Kentucky and had the trophies to prove it. The Preakness, Kentucky Derby, all the big races. I met him when I was making a house call to one of the breed farms. He was charming, sweet and before long, we started having an affair."

"There's nothing wrong with having an affair," he said.

She looked at Derek, at the patience banked in his gaze, and searched for the courage to finally tell him what a fool she'd been. "It wasn't just an affair. He asked me to marry him."

"And you accepted."

She nodded, feeling the guilt wash over her in waves. "Oh, yeah, I accepted."

"What happened, because you obviously didn't marry him."

"No. I couldn't have married him, but I didn't realize that at the time. I thought I was in love with him, but I don't know any longer."

Because he never made me feel the way you do.

She kept the thought to herself, because she didn't know how to classify her feelings for Derek. Although she'd hardly call it love, she did care about him—too much.

"For the six months of our engagement, I was blind," she admitted. Deaf, dumb *and* blind, she added silently. "There were signs right in front of me, and I didn't bother to stop and read them."

He frowned. "What signs?"

"Little things, really, things that bothered me, but I chose to ignore them because the great Nicholas Adams claimed to be in love with me. Like how he would take off for a week or two and not tell anyone, including me, where he'd gone. And how when he'd return, he'd always be just a little more distant. Then he'd change suddenly, and everything would be wonderful again.

"I even let him convince me to keep our engagement a secret. He worried that if the news got out, it could damage both of our careers—conflict of interest or some other stupid thing that I fell for because I trusted him. It took me six months to learn the truth."

His hand gently squeezed hers, and she took the gesture for the comfort he was offering.

"Was he seeing someone else?" he asked.

She shook her head. "Worse. He was married."

His oath was sharp and succinct.

"Married, with a child," she added, surprised by the hardness of her voice.

She was touched by the flash of anger that crossed his face. Derek. Her knight in shining armor, ready to defend his lady's honor.

"How'd you find out?"

"*Mrs.* Adams paid a surprise visit to Kentucky one afternoon," she said, then waited while the waiter replaced their uneaten salads with the entrées they'd ordered.

She pulled her hand from Derek's and picked up the fork to move the shrimp scampi around on her plate. "She'd traveled all the way from Ohio," she continued, not looking at him, "to celebrate her fifth wedding anniversary with her husband."

"I'm sorry, Syd," he offered consolingly.

She lifted her gaze to his, her heart twisting at the compassion in his eyes. "Don't be," she said, setting her fork on the edge of her plate. "It was my own stupidity. Anyway, I was called to the ranch of one of my clients, who had a three-year-old filly that was deep in training. She'd been slightly injured a couple of weeks before, and the owner needed clearance for Rainbow's Rocket before Nicholas could continue with her training. When I arrived, I saw Nicholas with this woman. He had his arm around her, so I asked Harold, Rainbow's owner, who the woman was, and he told me."

Derek pushed his plate forward and braced his arms on the table. He'd suspected, somewhere in the back of his mind, that perhaps someone had been unfaithful to Sydney, but he'd never have guessed she'd been engaged to a married man. Suddenly, her staunch refusal to talk about her time in Kentucky, and more importantly, the reason she repeatedly turned down his proposals of marriage, made a little more sense. He could understand her fears, but he wasn't the creep who'd cheated on his wife and lied to Syd.

"Adams's wife?" he asked, and received confirmation with her brief nod.

"Everything started to fall into place then. The long, unexplained absences. The distance. Keeping our engagement a secret. It had nothing to do with our careers or the supposed controversy or gossip."

She toyed with her rice pilaf. "At first, I thought maybe they were divorced and he just hadn't told me about his first marriage, which was upsetting enough. But then I saw his…daughter and I just knew. His wife had said something, and he leaned over and kissed her. I saw the way he looked at her, and it didn't matter if they were still married or divorced. I saw the same look he often gave me, and I knew what I had with Nicholas was nothing but a lie."

Derek studied her eyes, and he saw a glimpse of the pain and betrayal she'd suffered because of some creep who didn't know the meaning of the word *fidelity.* "Did you say anything?" he asked.

"Not then." She stabbed a piece of shrimp with her fork. "I was too hurt, and the last thing I wanted to do was hurt his wife and daughter, so I played it straight. I wanted to get in my car and leave, but I had a filly needing my attention, so I was forced to brave it out."

He couldn't see Syd running from anything, other than her feelings for him, so her facing the situation head-on didn't surprise him. "What did he do?"

She sniffed in derision, then popped the shrimp into her mouth. "Oh, he was a cool one," she said after a few minutes, a trace of iron in her voice. "Pretending there was nothing more between us than a professional relationship. God, it was so awful."

He reached out and slid his hand over hers. "I'm sorry you were hurt."

"I was more than hurt, Derek. I was ashamed."

He frowned. "Ashamed?" he asked incredulously. "You had nothing to be ashamed about."

She laughed, but the sound held no humor. "I was the classic 'other woman.'"

"You didn't know that. If you had, would you have continued to have an affair with this creep?"

"No. But I should have known. I should have paid more attention, listened to my instincts—they kept telling me something wasn't quite right. But I ignored them. I *chose* to ignore them because I thought I was in love, and I thought he loved me. I was gravely mistaken."

"Did you ever talk to him?"

"Oh, yeah. I listened to his line, then read him the riot act, packed up and came home."

"You can't keep letting one bad experience tarnish your views, Syd. You have to let it go." Because until she did leave the past where it belonged, he had serious doubts that he'd ever convince her they belonged together.

"Oh, I let it go, and learned a valuable lesson. Love is just an illusion."

He allowed a smile to lift his mouth. "That's where you're wrong."

"Am I?" she asked in a harsh whisper. She cast a quick glance around the restaurant, then turned her gaze back to him, spearing him with daggers of irritation. "Were you listening to what I just said?"

"I heard you." He strove for patience. If he gave in to the frustration nudging him, they'd only end up in another useless argument. "But love isn't your problem. Your problem is trust."

She set her fork aside and leaned back into the booth, crossing her arms over her chest. "Here we go again. What's your analysis this time, Sigmund?"

He struggled to ignore her sarcasm. "Whether or not you were really in love with this guy isn't the issue. You trusted him, and he betrayed that trust."

"And your point is?" she asked with a defiant tilt of her chin.

He wasn't fooled by her show of false bravado. The fear creeping into her eyes told him the truth. She was scared, damn scared that he was getting to the heart of the matter, and she had nowhere left to hide. "You're afraid to trust anyone."

The grin that curved her lips failed to chase away the sharp glint of suspicion in her gaze. "That's not true. I trust you."

"Do you now?" he asked with a lift of his brow.

Her grin faltered slightly. "Don't be silly," she said with a dismissing wave of her hand. She reached for the water glass and took a sip. "Of course, I do."

Dropping the linen napkin on the table beside his plate, he eased across the bench seat toward her. He felt her stiffen when he dipped his head to whisper low in her ear. "Show me."

Her breath caught, but she studied her plate, refusing to look at him. She set the water glass back on the table and picked up her fork.

"Trust, Syd." He nuzzled the slender column of her neck with brief, featherlight kisses. Male satisfaction surged through him when she trembled. "Trust *me*."

She leaned back and looked at him. Wild, caught-in-the-headlights fear clouded her eyes. "Derek—"

Before she could argue, he kissed her. He cupped her neck in his hand and gently ran his thumb over her erratic pulse. He tormented her mouth with lazy sweeps of his tongue until he felt the soft give of her slender body as she leaned into him, surrendering to what her heart and body knew as the truth, but her mind was too stubborn to accept.

He ended the kiss and looked into her eyes. Soft, luminous eyes filled with the first stirring of awareness. "Trust me," he said again. "I won't ever hurt you. I won't ever lie to you. But you have to trust me."

"I—"

He placed a finger over her lips to still the arguments. "Do something for me."

"What?" she asked, her voice a choked whisper of sound.

Derek knew he was going to regret this, but he'd jumped on a runaway train knowing full well he could end up in a head-on collision with heartache. But he had to make her realize she *could* trust him. With her life, with her soul, and with her heart.

"Take off your panties," he said, and had the feeling the emergency brake just snapped off in his hand.

9

SYDNEY'S HEART skidded to a halt, then resumed at a maddening pace. "You want me to do what?"

She glanced around the darkened restaurant to make sure no one had heard his outrageous request, and was relieved when the other diners paid them no notice.

She turned to face him, but the words denying his request died on her tongue. The grin of a scoundrel curved his lips, and there was something dark and just a little dangerous in his eyes that had her wondering how far he'd take this little game.

"Take off your panties and hand them to me," he demanded in a husky rumble.

She swallowed past the heady rush of excitement welling in her throat. "Why?"

He slipped the tip of his finger beneath the thin strap of her dress, following a path over her shoulder, stopping a breath away from the swell of her breast. "Don't you trust me?"

She looked at him, and the passion smoldering in his darkened gaze. "I...I thought...I don't know," she finally stammered. Did she trust him? Could she?

With the warmth of his finger, he teased the swell of her breast while his gaze held her mesmerized. Her nipples hardened in response, straining against the cool silk of her dress.

"Do it, sweetheart. Show me you trust me."

Her insides clenched at the faintly wicked gleam in his eyes that was pure temptation. A combination of anxiety and excitement shot through her, making her feel a trifle reckless and a whole lot naughty.

She shrugged, as if stripping off her underwear in a public restaurant was something she did whenever the mood struck. Keeping her gaze locked with his, she gave him what she hoped was a sultry look and lifted her bottom off the seat. With a shimmy and a corresponding wiggle, she slowly slipped out of her black lace panties. His gaze darkened, stirring the flames inside her that were never far from igniting whenever he was near. After another quick glance around the restaurant, she gave the lace a final tug, slid the panties over her stockings and held them beneath the tablecloth. Her heart pounded and heat pooled in her tummy. Cool silk cradled her bottom and brushed against her hips. The only thing she could think of that'd be more erotic would be Derek's hands sliding over her.

He took her panties from her and slowly dragged his thumb over the scrap of black lace, then rubbed the material between his fingers. There was something sensual and terribly erotic in the action. The heat pooling in her tummy spread outward through her limbs, like hot lava spilling over the side of a volcano. She felt achy inside, and would lay odds that had been his intent.

"Now what?" she asked, wondering if she'd have the nerve to follow through on whatever he had planned next in this little fantasy.

"Now we finish our dinner." He stuffed her panties in the pocket of his jacket and turned his attention to his meal.

He expected her to eat! She narrowed her eyes. "What kind of game are you playing?"

He carefully removed a piece of lobster from its shell. "I'm not playing any games with you, Syd. I'm just trying to show you that you *can* trust me."

"By asking me to strip in public?" she asked in a harsh whisper.

That rascal grin was back again. He dipped the lobster into the small tub of drawn butter, swirled it around, then held the delectable meat to her lips. "Bite?"

She leaned forward and he brushed the lobster gently against her lips. She opened her mouth, but he held it a breath away. "Just hold it on your tongue for a minute."

She arched her brow, wondering again what he was up to, but complied just the same. He was, after all, offering her lobster.

"What did you feel?" he asked in that husky rumble of sexuality that had her tingling all over.

"Butter, seafood."

"Not taste. Textures."

Okay, she thought. *Two can play this game.* "Warm. Succulent." She gave him a wicked grin of her own. "Wet."

Her grin widened when he shifted in his seat. "You play dirty," he said.

She plucked a piece of shrimp from her plate and held it toward his lips. "You started it."

He laughed softly, the intimate sound rumbling over her nerve endings as if he'd touched her physically. "Tell me what *you* feel," she demanded, offering him the shrimp.

He grasped her wrist, rubbing his thumb over her pulse. "Hot." He drew lazy circles on the underside of her wrist, his gaze holding hers with cocky self-assurance. "Slick. And moist," he added.

"Is it...stiff?" she asked wickedly.

Still holding her wrist, he guided her hand beneath the table. "You tell me."

Before she could even think about what she was doing, or be shocked by her own brazen behavior, she slid her hand up the smooth silk-blend leg of his trousers to his thigh. Her gaze held his. Hot. Intense. Filled with a desire so raw it rattled what was left of her composure.

She reveled in the delicious abandon, the danger, and God help her, a need so explicit and urgent it rocked her. With deliberate slowness, she eased her hand further up his thigh to cup his *very* aroused sex in her hand.

He sucked in a sharp breath.

Her heart rate accelerated and a tiny thrill of pleasure shot through her.

"We need to get out of here," she whispered softly. "Or they'll either be throwing us out or having us arrested for lewd and libidinous conduct."

"What about dessert?" he asked, his hand sliding over hers and easing her searching fingers away from his arousal.

"Professor," she said, using the sexiest tone she could muster. She leaned toward him, intentionally brushing her breasts against his arm as she rested her chin on his shoulder to whisper seductively in his ear. "You're just gonna have to trust me."

HOW IN THE HELL did she do it? Somehow, somewhere he'd lost control, and she'd grabbed it so fast he hadn't even seen her seductive and all too arousing counterstrike coming.

Derek shifted his gaze from the roadway to her and back again. She sat looking out the window at the lights of the city, as if she hadn't just twisted him up in knots so tight he thought he might spontaneously combust. She kept her legs crossed, her foot bouncing slightly in time to the soft rock music on the stereo. He couldn't forget that her panties were tucked safely in his pocket.

Another glance and his gaze zeroed in on the barest hint of lace at the tops of her stockings, where her slip of a dress ended. The gentle sway of her hips when they'd left the restaurant had just about had him coming out of his skin knowing there was nothing between her smooth flesh and the black silk clinging to her curves.

Sweet heaven. He was in trouble. Deep, deep trouble. His own tortuous path to hell was paved in her delectable body, and his solemn promise of temporary celibacy was close to being forgotten. How was he going to turn away from her tonight, when all he wanted to do was carry her off to bed and make love to her until they were both too exhausted to move?

He had no answer by the time he pulled into her driveway and turned off the engine. With his arm slung over the steering wheel, he turned to face her. The look in her eyes held him spellbound, conveying exactly what she wanted.

Sex.

Hot, damp bodies, tangled sheets, anything goes sex.

His body answered her siren's call, hardening so fast he ached with a powerful need to have her. She was making him crazy, and making him forget every one of his good intentions.

Before he climbed into the back seat and dragged her with him like an oversexed teenager, he slipped from the vehicle. Warm, sultry air hit him square in the face, and he bit back a frustrated curse. He needed cool air. Hell, he needed a cold shower!

He opened her door and took hold of her hand, helping her from the Explorer. Her eyes held his as she slowly slid from the seat. Did every look, every move, every breath she took have to remind him of sex?

Hot, damp bodies, tangled sheets, anything goes sex.

She strode past him, her hips swaying provocatively as she led the way up the brick path to her door. Derek loosened the tie that suddenly felt like a noose around his neck.

"Coming?" she asked with a glance over her shoulder hot enough to melt the polar ice caps.

He nearly groaned at the sinfully throaty note in her voice.

He slipped off his sport coat and tossed it on the seat she'd just vacated, then slammed the door to the Explorer. His arms ached to hold her. His body ached to have her.

"Trouble," he muttered, and walked up the brick path toward her. "The woman is trouble, squared. No, cubed."

She leaned against the porch railing, her hands gripping the wood behind her. If she intended for her breasts to press against the thin silk covering her body, then she'd met her goal. Even in the moonlight, he could see the outline of those perfectly shaped globes, and his hands itched to test their weight in his palms.

He stopped in front of her and braced his hands on either side of her, trapping her within the heat of his body. Her lips parted and she tipped her head back, waiting for him to kiss her.

He did, clamping his mouth over hers in demanding possession.

Her mouth went soft and hot in response. She kissed him like a woman who knew what she wanted and had no qualms about making her intentions clear. The sweep of her tongue wasn't gentle, but equally demanding, letting him know she wanted him in the most elemental way possible. He pressed closer, needing the feel of her soft curves against him.

He chased her tongue, slipping inside the moist haven, taking in the hot and all too tempting taste of her.

She was so sweet. She was heaven and temptation all rolled into one, and he didn't know if he had the strength to walk away from her. His stupid rule be damned, he thought. He wanted her, wanted her in the worst possible way, and from the way she was pressing against him and making sweet mewling sounds in the back of her throat, she wanted him just as desperately.

He groaned, a deep, rough sound that made her squirm against him. The sounds of the city floated on the evening breeze, but the world around him receded until there was only the two of them, their desire and need driving them both closer to the edge.

The sound of a blaring horn drifted to him through the sensual fog clouding his mind. Sydney pulled back. "Not here." Slipping her fingers over his tie, she tugged and he obediently followed her out of the path of oncoming headlights to a darkened, sheltered corner of the porch.

He had to stop before things went too far. He should, but he couldn't, not with the need crashing through them both overriding his good intentions.

"I want you. Now, Derek."

"Easy, sweetheart," he whispered, while her hot, damp mouth trailed kisses along his throat.

His fingers brushed her thigh and slipped beneath the hem of her dress. She whimpered, and he responded to the force of her desire as he smoothed his hand over her thigh and caressed her damp curls.

Sydney arched her hips toward the teasing brush of his fingers against her slick folds. She couldn't ever remembering needing someone as much as she needed Derek. Her desire went beyond sex, went beyond her body's cry for release. It went deeper, to a place she'd thought safe—her heart.

The realization should have had her running as far away from him as she could get, but she couldn't move. Instead, she clung to him and whispered erotic promises that had his breath coming in short, sharp pants.

With her dress eased up, the warm, sultry air brushed against her skin, adding heat to his already burning touch. His mouth sought hers in a kiss so deep and hot and wet she nearly unraveled. His fingers slipped inside her, and he groaned. "You're so wet," he muttered against her mouth. "So sweet."

He made a sound, a deep, rough sound that bordered on a growl, and then he pulled her into a storm of sensation. He made love to her mouth until she lost track of everything around her but the tension coiling low in her tummy and the fire racing through her veins. He stroked, teased and showed her that he was more than familiar with the secrets of her body. He knew just how to make her come apart in his arms, and he carried her there.

Her body tensed, closing around his fingers as she edged toward the climax he promised. She bowed against him, and he caught her before she slipped over the edge, his mouth capturing her cries of release as she rode the crest toward sweet completion.

She clung to him, breathing hard, certain her heart and body would never be the same again.

Tenderly, he straightened her dress, then held her against him while her senses returned to normal. His own breathing was unsteady as he stroked her back and kissed the dampness at her temple.

She couldn't help be thrilled by the acquaintance with this dangerous, reckless side of Derek. He'd awoken a side of herself she hadn't known existed, one that reveled in the danger.

She looked into his eyes, and for once, the tenderness in them failed to frighten her. Maybe she did trust him. Just a little. "Stay the night."

"No, sweetheart," he said, his voice filled with regret. "Tonight I want you to think about us."

Puzzled, she turned her head slightly to the side. "Us?"

He eased his hands up to cradle her face in his warm palms. He kissed her again, slow and gentle, then lifted his head. "I love you, Sydney. But until you can tell me you love me, this is as far as we go."

She stared at him, unable to believe what she was hearing. He had to be joking. At least she hoped so. "That's...that's sexual blackmail!"

He shrugged and dropped his hands to his sides. "You can't keep using me for sex."

Her jaw fell open, then she snapped it shut. "I'm not using you for sex," she cried in outrage. Of all the ridiculous...

He took a step back and shoved his hands into the pockets of his trousers. "I don't know what guy in his right mind would turn down the chance to make love to such a beautiful and exciting woman with no strings attached, but I'm into strings, sweetheart. I want you. But I want all of you."

He was asking for the impossible. Dammit! Hadn't he heard a word she'd said at dinner? Wasn't he listening when she'd told him about the horrendous mistake she'd made believing in Nicholas? True, Derek wasn't Nicholas. In fact, Nicholas didn't even come close to being half the man that Derek was, but how could she give her heart to another, only to have it trampled again? She cared about him—too much—but not the way he wanted. He wanted her love, and she just didn't have it to give.

"I can't," she said, her voice barely a whisper.

He turned and walked down the steps, then stopped to turn back to face her. "You can. But you're just gonna have to trust me."

The regret clouding his eyes nearly broke her heart. Which was impossible, since she didn't have a heart to break.

SATURDAY MORNINGS were usually relatively quiet, but for some reason, every dog, cat, hamster and pet goldfish had come down with one ailment after another. And to top off the craziness, Rachel had to call off because one of her daughters had been injured during softball practice. Her arm had swollen during the night and now Rachel feared Lori might have a broken bone, requiring a visit to the emergency room. Sydney had told her assistant not to worry, that she could handle things, but that had been before the madness of the unexpected morning rush.

Normally she reveled in the craziness, but considering she'd only managed an hour, two at most, of sleep the previous night, she longed for the usual quiet of the Saturday morning routine. By ten o'clock, she was ready to send the dozen patients in the waiting room home and close the clinic doors. A rottweiler in for a hip X-ray had growled at her. Normally a growling dog didn't bother her, but considering her emotions were running in high gear, she'd taken the dog's attitude personally and had actually broken down and cried. Mrs. Cushing's pregnant, and obviously cranky, Scottish terrier, Maggie, had snapped at her, and for relieving a cantankerous Siamese of a particularly nasty hair ball, she'd received a long, deep gash on the back of her hand as a thank-you.

She'd just finished spitting out a feather from a temperamental and molting African Gray in for a wing clipping when the back of her neck tingled. She glanced over her shoulder, not surprised to find Derek leaning against the doorjamb of the examination room.

"Thank goodness you showed up," she said. Considering the morning she was having, she would have been grateful to see Attila the Hun, but Derek would just have to do. The African Gray started flapping his wings again, sending a flurry of feathers dancing around her. "I could really use an extra hand."

She'd upbraid him later for leaving her achy with need and thinking about him all night as he'd so arrogantly prophesied. Right now, she needed help with the grouchy, exotic bird.

He sauntered into the examination room and

gave her a cocksure grin that had her wanting to snap his head off. "Glad to see me, huh?"

"Almost," she muttered. Contrary to the actions of her patients that morning, she wasn't about to bite the hand willing to lend itself in aid. Instead, she rolled her eyes and showed him how to hold the bird so she could get the wings clipped and move on to the next patient.

Once the bird was safely back in his travel carrier, she gave Derek the *Reader's Digest* version of the operation of the outside office. She expected chaos, but surprisingly for the last two hours that the clinic remained open, he kept things in control and her busy with a steady stream of patients, from simple vaccinations to the heartbreaking task of having to tell Mabel Farmer that the French poodle that had been her constant companion for the past twenty years was going blind.

By the time the last patient left the clinic an hour past her usual closing time, Sydney was exhausted. She sank into the peach vinyl chair in the examination room, dropped her head back and closed her eyes.

"Rough morning."

She lifted her lashes and glared at Derek. "Do your students ever complain about the pace you keep?"

He chuckled, and if she'd had the energy, she would have thrown something at him. She felt like something one of her patients buried in the yard, while he had the audacity to look fresh, clean and as if he'd had a good night's sleep.

"Janet DeYoung called from the airport," he

said, checking the note in his hands. "Something about your promising to deliver Rocky?"

Sydney groaned. "The golden retriever I've been boarding all week. I forgot all about having to take him home today."

"You look beat. I'll take him home."

As much as she'd love to take a hot shower and crawl into bed for the rest of the afternoon, she couldn't shirk her responsibilities. "Derek, I don't think—"

"Look, you're beat. You have no business getting behind the wheel. It's not like I don't know how to handle a dog, for crying out loud."

"Are you sure?" she asked, letting the enticement of a shower and long nap override her better judgment.

"Positive," he said, then pulled her to her feet. "You write down the directions, and I'll load him into the truck."

Instead of arguing, she took him up on his offer. Ten minutes later, Rocky sat in the passenger seat of Derek's Explorer. "Bronson's going to be jealous," she said, scratching the dog behind the ears. "He always has to sit in the back seat."

"He'll get over it." Derek slipped his arms around her and pulled her close.

She told herself the only reason she didn't tell him to keep his hands to himself was because she was so exhausted; it had absolutely nothing to do with the crazy tingling rippling through her. "Uh, speaking of Bronson," she said, hoping to get her mind off his embrace and all the delightful things she wanted to do to him, "please tell me you took out his stitches."

He gave her another one of those tolerant looks. "I told you I can handle a dog. Now, how about dinner?" he asked.

She leaned back and gave him a skeptical look. "I don't think I could handle another dinner like last night's," she said wryly.

His answering chuckle sent a delightful warmth flowing through her. "I was thinking of throwing some steaks on the grill."

"That'd be nice. But you can't cook," she reminded him, and eased out of his arms.

He frowned. "Men barbecue, they don't cook."

She considered turning down his offer, but during the long hours after he'd left her last night, she'd come to a few conclusions. By dawn, when she'd finally given up trying to sleep, she'd decided she couldn't keep Derek dangling. She needed to be honest with him and let him know in no uncertain terms that as much as she was touched by his offer, she wouldn't ever marry him. It was time he stopped his backward proposals and attempts to show her what her life could be like if she agreed to be his wife. She wanted him to be her friend...and lover. She'd sworn she'd never marry, and while he tempted her beyond reason, she just couldn't bring herself to take that final step. He was a part of her life, and she hoped he always would be, but their relationship would never go any further than it already had.

She let out a puff of breath that ruffled her bangs. "I'll be there about seven."

He leaned toward her to kiss her goodbye, but she turned and gave Rocky her attention, knowing that if Derek kissed her, she just might change her mind, and her resolve.

And that was something she couldn't do.

DEREK IDLED down one side street after another, but after an hour and a half, he hadn't caught a single glimpse of the prized golden retriever. He still didn't know how it had happened. One minute, the dog had been hanging his head out the window, sniffing the air while the wind whipped his long ears, and the next, he'd been gone.

Sydney was going to skin him alive. She'd trusted him, and he let her down. God, why now? Why when he was so close to convincing her that they could be happy together, did something like this have to happen?

He circled the block one last time, then having no other choice, he headed toward Sydney's with the bad news.

He let himself into the cottage. She was asleep on the sofa, curled on her side, wrapped in a soft, pink chenille robe, one hand tucked near her cheek, the other resting protectively over her tummy, over her baby. Their baby. He couldn't help wondering if he'd ever get over that strange sense of awe that the thought of her swollen with his child brought him. He didn't think so.

His heart constricted in his chest. Even though he'd grown up in a single-parent household, he'd always believed in happily-ever-afters and finding that one special woman to spend the rest of his life with, but he'd never known it was possible to love another person as much as he loved her.

After he told her that he'd lost Rocky, she'd probably never speak to him again.

He crouched in front of her and gently rocked her shoulder. "Syd?"

Her lashes fluttered and he looked into her sleep-filled green eyes. "Sweetheart, I've got some bad news."

Her brow furrowed and her hand automatically pressed against her tummy.

"Sweetheart, I lost Rocky."

Her brow puckered as his words registered. She sat up and stared at him. "You what?"

"I don't know what happened. One minute he was sitting in the passenger seat and the next he was gone."

"Derek, no. Please tell me you're joking."

The disappointment in her voice slid around his heart and squeezed. "I'm sorry, Syd."

She shot off the sofa and started to pace the living room. Her hands clenched into fists at her sides, and her profile wasn't the least bit sympathetic. She stopped and swung around to face him, but the ringing of the telephone kept her from lashing him with the angry words he was sure resided on the tip of her tongue.

She crossed the room and snagged the cordless phone. He winced when she forcefully punched the button to receive the call. "Yes," she snapped.

After a moment, the tension left her body and she sagged against the back of the sofa. "You're more than welcome," she said into the phone. "No, he was no trouble at all."

She cast Derek a look over her shoulder and shook her head, disbelief in her emerald gaze.

"That's fine, Janet. No, I'm glad everything worked out."

She punched the button to disconnect the call and tossed the phone on the sofa. When she turned to face him, the disbelief was still evident in her features. "Don't ask me how it happened, but you are one lucky man, Dr. Buchanan."

He straightened. "What do you mean?" he asked cautiously.

"That was Janet DeYoung. She was calling to apologize for being so late, and to thank me for leaving Rocky in the backyard for her."

"I don't understand." He'd been at least two miles from the DeYoung place. How was it possible?

She looked at him as if she couldn't believe his luck. "Rocky was waiting for her when she got home."

"Well, I'll be damned," he said, grinning like a fool. He'd gotten lucky, and he knew it.

Oh yeah, he thought, despite the scowl on Sydney's face. She was going to be his. With luck like his, how could he possibly not win the heart of the woman he loved?

10

SYDNEY TUCKED the red cotton tank top into the waistband of her tan shorts. In the not too distant future, waistbands would be a thing of the past, she thought, examining her profile in the full-length mirror. She rested her hand against her still flat abdomen. From the books she'd read, she could start showing as early as three months, or as late as five or six months. She hoped for three.

After pulling her hair back and securing the mass of curls with the gold clip she always wore, she applied a minimum of makeup and was ready to leave for Derek's. She still couldn't believe how fortunate they'd been that Rocky had by some miracle arrived at the DeYoung house. Janet would have been heartbroken if her companion disappeared, and Sydney would have felt terrible, too. Besides, the cost to replace the multichampioned golden retriever and stud dog would have put a major dent in her savings account. If she didn't put a stop to Derek's good intentions soon, she'd either go broke or crazy.

She slipped into a pair of strappy leather sandals, picked up her purse, then left for Derek's. He lived only a few blocks away, across the street from her childhood home. By the time she pulled in front of the little white frame house, with its neatly trimmed lawn and concrete walkway bordered on both sides by Mrs. Buchanan's colorful roses, she still hadn't decided how to approach him about their relationship.

She ignored her nagging conscience, which was trying to tell her she was making a mistake of monstrous proportions. She cared about Derek, but she couldn't let herself fall in love with him. To do so would bring an end to a friendship that spanned twenty-two years, and that wasn't something she was willing to trade for a few years of great sex and companionship until the resentment of raising a child that might not be his finally drove him away. At least this way, they would always be friends.

She hoped.

She slipped from the truck and heard Bronson's welcoming bark as she walked up the driveway to the back gate. "Hey there, pal," she called to the dog when she flipped open the latch.

The big, red Dobie's stubby tail moved back and forth, his thick back end wiggling with excitement. Once Bronson stopped roaming around her in circles, she followed the dog into the backyard. She stilled at the edge of the garage when she spied Derek. Just the sight of him had the power to take her breath away. He stood with his back to her, giving her a perfect view of his denim-covered backside. His hands were braced against the green-and-white-checked plastic tablecloth on the picnic table, his forearms thick with corded muscle and sinew. His head bent as he read the directions on a bag of charcoal, a lock of dark hair falling over his forehead. Just looking at him stroked her feminine senses.

She shook the thought from her mind. She'd accepted his dinner invitation for the sole purpose of putting an end to his misguided belief that they should be married.

"For the safety of the neighborhood," she called out as she crossed the lawn toward him, "maybe I should buy you one of those fancy electric barbecues for your birthday."

He looked up, and her heart faltered in her chest. A drop-dead killer grin tugged at his lips, and those sexy eyes slid over her, lingering on places that had her insides fluttering with anticipation.

"I'm running a little behind. I gave Bronson a bath, but he decided he wanted to play rather than cooperate."

That explained the damp concrete of the covered patio. She set her purse on the picnic bench. "Anything I can do to help?" *And save dinner,* she thought humorously.

"Everything else is done," he said, ripping open the bag of charcoal. He hefted the bag in his arms. Her breath caught when the material of his T-shirt tightened over his biceps, and she itched to trail her hands over the iron-hard skin she knew would feel rough and smooth at the same time.

"Just relax," he said, dumping charcoal into the base of the barbecue.

Relax? As if that were possible. How was she supposed to relax when all she could think about was touching him?

She eased into the chaise longue and slipped off her sunglasses, setting them on the round redwood table while Derek arranged the briquettes in the bottom of the grill and started the fire without alarming the neighborhood. Bronson walked over and nudged her hand, begging for affection. She took advantage of Derek being otherwise occupied and double-checked to make sure he'd removed all of Bronson's stitches.

Derek disappeared into the house, then returned a moment later with two tall, frosted glasses of lemonade. He handed her one, then pulled a matching chair over and sat. "Syd, I am sorry about what happened this afternoon with Rocky. I still don't know how it happened."

She didn't either, but at least everything had worked out. For that she was grateful.

"Forget about it," she said, then lifted the glass to her lips to sip hesitantly. She lifted a brow in surprise. "This is good," she said, then took another drink.

He gave her one of those tolerant looks she'd become used to lately. "What did you expect? Seeds and no sugar?"

She laughed and set the glass on the table next to her sunglasses. "Neither."

His good-natured grin made her pulse beat just a tad faster. "Liar." He set his glass next to hers and looked at her intently. "I've been meaning to ask you, when's your next appointment with the doctor?"

She frowned. "Not for another two weeks. Why?" she asked cautiously.

He shrugged. "I'd like to go with you."

She let out the breath she hadn't even realized she'd been holding. "Derek, I—"

He lifted his hand to stop her before she could tell him she didn't think that was a good idea. He might be interested in the baby now, but once they learned the truth, that the baby was the product of the sperm clinic's daddy-to-go, his interest would wane. She'd rather he not bother and save them both a lot of heartache.

His dark brows lowered in a scowl. "Why don't you just accept it, Syd? This baby means as much to me as it does to you."

She sucked in a deep breath and let it out slowly in an effort to keep her cool. Since she planned on having a serious conversation with him later about their "future," it wouldn't do her any good to turn all cranky and surly now. "Because it might not be yours," she stated in a reasonable tone just shy of patronizing. "Why can't you accept that?"

He stood and looked down at her, frustration hardening his features. "What difference docs it make who the father is?" he returned, planting his hands on his hips. "I love you, and this baby is a part of you. That's enough for me, Syd. Why can't *you* accept that?"

She didn't think anyone had ever shouted an *I love you* at her before.

"You say that now." She met his stormy gaze and fought to maintain a calm she was far from feeling. She was starting to feel cornered, and she didn't like the panic splintering through her one bit.

"What happens five years from now? I've

seen—" No. She wouldn't go there. Derek wasn't Nicholas, but even the truth of that statement couldn't stop her fear that if she let him into that part of her life, he'd eventually come to resent her and her child.

She swung her feet to the ground and stood. "You know what? I don't want to argue about it. I've already made my feelings clear." She stepped around him and headed toward the house.

He dogged her heels. "So have I," he said, opening the screen door for her. "You're going to have to accept it sooner or later."

She stopped in the doorway and looked at him, hating that she was the cause of the angry cast to his handsome face. "Can we talk about something else?" she suggested. "I don't want to spoil our evening by arguing."

The furrows between his brows softened. "You're right," he said after a moment. "Let's not fight about this."

She forced out a relaxing breath and walked into the cozy kitchen where she'd spent so much of her life. Memories flooded her: helping Mrs. Buchanan frost dozens and dozens of Christmas cookies for PTA bake sales, Derek quizzing her for a science exam, her helping him write an English term paper on *Romeo and Juliet*, and the myriad conversations they'd shared during the years. She thought about how he always kept her favorite chocolate doughnuts on hand, how he knew that she liked only three marshmallows in her hot cocoa along with an extra splash of milk to cool it, and that she preferred sour cream and chives to butter on her baked potatoes. He always knew just what she liked or wanted without having to ask. Simple things that made little or no difference in the big scheme of things, and things she was embarrassed to admit she'd always taken for granted.

Until now.

Now the knowledge filled her with a sense of panic. Her heart beat heavily in her chest. She stepped up to the sink and wrapped her fingers around the ceramic-tiled edge. Had she somehow been in love with Derek all these months and not even realized it? She remembered her mother once making a special trip to three different markets for some particular food that her father adored. When she'd asked her mother why she went to so much trouble, she'd told her she did it because it made her father happy. At the time, she'd thought her mother was crazy wasting all that time running all over Seattle, but now she understood that love wasn't about roses and chocolate, or Shakespearean poetry declaring undying platitudes of emotion.

No, she thought, love was the little things. The moving tons of brick to get rid of those pesky weeds she always complained about, keeping chocolate doughnuts on hand because they were her favorite snack food, or remembering how she liked her baked potatoes.

There was so much about him she knew, too, and things she did because she knew he'd appreciate them. There was the way she'd reorganize the Sunday paper because he liked to read the sports section first, followed by the comics, and finally the business section, or how he liked his popcorn without butter or his eggs cooked once-over-lightly. He preferred bacon to sausage and liked powdered sugar on his waffles rather than maple syrup. She never cared much for tomatoes, but she always bought them because he liked them with just about everything. And he liked those little baby dill pickles instead of the sweet ones she preferred.

"Syd? You okay?"

The concern in his voice caught her attention. She loosened her grip on the tile and turned, pinning on a weak grin. "I'm fine," she lied, then reached into the cabinet to pull out a couple of plates. Thirty minutes ago, she'd been determined to tell him their relationship could go no further. They were friends, and friends they would remain.

Now she wasn't so sure.

DEREK SWATTED another mosquito. He'd bought one of those candles that claimed to keep the bloodsucking creatures at bay, but the darned thing was turning out to be useless against the invading army. And worse, they hadn't even bothered to pester Sydney. He, on the other hand, felt like the bestselling entrée on the food chain.

The back door screen squeaked, and he glanced over his shoulder to see Sydney carrying a serving tray with plates, silverware and the baked potatoes still wrapped in foil. God, he could get used to this.

She walked over to the picnic table, set down the tray, and started arranging their plates. She leaned over, and he caught sight of her very feminine posterior. His mouth went dry when she reached across the table, the low cut of her top giving him a perfect glimpse of her full breasts.

He cleared his throat and searched for something to say that didn't include a proposition to slip into a horizontal position. "What about names?" he asked, forcing himself to focus on transferring the steaks from the grill to the metal serving tray.

She laid out silverware and glanced up at him. "I haven't given it much thought."

He gave her a skeptical look. He knew enough about women to know they started thinking about silly things like baby names once they were old enough to figure out that they were the ones responsible for giving birth.

She gave him a heart-stopping grin. "Okay," she said, laughing. "I have thought about it. Sabrina or Simon."

"Simon?" He cringed.

"Simon was my grandfather's name," she said defensively, and sat while he placed a New York strip on each of their plates.

"With a name like Simon," he said, setting the tray aside, "the poor little guy's bound to get beat up on the playground at least once a week."

She tore open the foil surrounding her baked potato and added a hefty dose of sour cream. "What do you suggest? Something macho, like Buck?"

He shook his head, removing the foil from his own potato. "Not a good idea. Rhymes with—"

She gasped and gave him a sharp, chiding glance. "Never mind," she said in a tone that would have made any schoolteacher proud. "What about Theodore?"

"Theodore?"

Was she nuts? Everything about Theodore and Simon spelled "nerd" as far as he was concerned. He had a pretty darned good understanding of basic genetics, and considering that he and Sydney had always been straight-A students with little effort, that meant their kid's chances of being an academic were high. "You looking to give the kid a complex or what?" he asked, eliminating another Dracula descendant intent on making him its latest victim.

"There is nothing wrong with Theodore," she said haughtily. "The name didn't hurt Theodore Roosevelt, ya know."

He shook his head and swatted at another hovering mosquito. "Sounds like one of the Chipmunks."

She giggled, her green eyes filling with laughter. He'd give anything to see her like this all the time.

"At least I didn't suggest Alvin."

He chuckled, cutting into his steak. "Wanna try again, Doc?"

"Sloan's a nice name. Or maybe Steven."

Steve Buchanan. He liked the sound of that, except convincing her to use his last name could turn out to be another battle. But one worth fighting. And winning.

He frowned when a mosquito bit into his flesh. "Aren't you getting attacked?" he asked, shooing away yet another bloodsucking creature. He set aside his fork and listened for the irritating buzz of the next attack.

She shook her head and sliced into the steak. "Not at all."

He waited for the buzz to move nearer, then he struck, bringing his hand down on the table with a loud thud.

Sydney jumped, and reached for her lemonade, but wasn't able to save it. The glass toppled, running over the tablecloth and pouring over the side.

Lemonade splashed on Bronson's head, who slept beneath the edge of the table. The big dog yelped and darted away, running straight into the barbecue.

The grill tipped, then fell over, tossing hot coals on the grass, the cushioned chairs and the patio. With another yelp, Bronson bolted toward the white Explorer and leapt into the back seat through the open window.

"Oh, my God," Sydney cried, rushing after Bronson. "Derek, get the hose!"

It took only seconds before the plastic covering on the chairs melted and the fiber filling burst into flames.

Derek raced for the garden hose. He cranked the faucet to high and gave the nozzle a sharp twist. Water rushed out of the hose and he doused the flames before they spread, then hosed down the still smoldering coals scattered over the patio and small section of lawn.

"He's okay," Sydney said. "Just a little scared—"

She gasped as Derek turned, taking the hose

with him and hitting her square in the chest with the icy water.

He dropped the hose and reached for her.

The hose took on a life of its own, snaking like one of those water toys kids used in the summer to keep cool, spraying them both.

She gave a carefree laugh and managed to tackle the hose, but not before they were both soaked clear to the skin. She took over, making sure the remaining coals were doused, then twisted the nozzle to staunch the flow of water.

"Here," she said, holding the hose out to him, humor lacing her voice. "I think it's safe now."

Whether she was talking about the coals or the hose, he didn't know, and quite honestly, he didn't care. He stood there, dripping wet, gaping at her like a lovesick fool. She'd lost her hair clip, and her hair hung around her shoulders, water dripping from the ends and adding to the moisture of her soaked red tank top. The garment clung to her, outlining her full breasts, and he could have sworn her nipples beaded into hard little crests right before his eyes.

She cleared her throat and looked over at the picnic table. "Our dinner's ruined," she said, glancing back at him. When she saw his expression, confusion lit her gaze, and she shivered.

Her shiver brought him out of his trance. "A hot shower will warm you up," he said, slinging the hose over the back of a ruined deck chair. "Then what do you say we order a pizza?"

The confusion was still in her eyes, but she nodded, then preceded him into the house.

He waited until he heard the shower running,

then placed a call for pizza delivery and walked back outside to assure himself Bronson was okay. The dog was snoring, rather loudly, and spread across the back seat of his Explorer. Not finding any good reason to disturb the dog, he left him to sleep, then returned to the house, intent on getting out of his soaked clothes.

He went down the hall to the laundry room, dripping water on the carpet, then shucked off his jeans and T-shirt. Wearing nothing but his briefs, he headed back down the hall to the bathroom, where he kept the extra towels.

He listened at the door and heard Sydney's off-tune humming, then figured he could slip in, grab a towel from the cabinet, and slip out again without her noticing. He opened the door, saw the shadow of her perfect body silhouetted against the shower curtain...and promptly left his plan in the hallway.

To hell with good intentions, he thought. He pulled off his briefs and his no-commitment-no-sex rule and kicked them both aside, then grabbed the shower curtain and slid it along the metal pole with only one thought on his mind: to make love to her until they were both too exhausted to move, and then make love to her again and again all night long.

Sydney whirled around at the sound of metal scraping metal, her hands automatically shifting to cover body parts. Derek stood on the other side of the tub, the white plastic shower curtain gripped in his huge hand, and an intense heat burning in his eyes.

She let her hands fall to her sides and held her

breath, willing him to step into the bathtub with her. He did, and she smiled, then waited for him to jerk the curtain closed before slipping her arms around his neck and pressing her water-soaked body against his.

He reached behind her and took the bar of soap from the holder. "Turn around," he demanded hoarsely.

She did, never breaking contact with his body. A soft moan escaped her lips when his soap-slicked hands slid over her shoulders, down her arms, then slipped around to her waist and upward to cup her breasts. She didn't even attempt to swallow the sharp gasp of pleasure when his thumbs brushed rhythmically over her nipples, the crests beading tight beneath his touch. She reached upward, her hands cupping the back of his neck until her backside was pressed intimately against his rigid arousal. His hands left her breasts and drew lazy patterns over her stomach, sliding sensuously lower until he brushed her inner thighs. She lowered her hands and covered his, urging him to touch her, to explore the part of her she knew was hot and ready for him, the place where his touch would take her over the edge and into sweet oblivion.

Instead he spun her around and clamped his mouth over hers in a tongue-tangling kiss that curled her toes. The hair on his chest grazed her sensitized breasts, his firm arousal pressed against her stomach, and she brazenly arched against him. He answered her body's call by easing her back against the tiled wall away from the spray of hot water, his big hands sliding over her, searching, teasing, igniting the fires of her soul.

His mouth left hers, kissing and tasting, first her throat, then her breasts and then lower, and lower still as he moved down her stomach. He crouched in front of her, and the water pounded against his back. He ignored it, and stopped at her navel, then dipped his tongue inside. She didn't think she'd ever felt anything more erotic, until his roving mouth continued downward and settled over the center of her heat.

She eased out a hiss of breath and dug her hands into his wet, dark hair. She tilted her head back, resting it against the tile, and moaned softly as too many sensations to name erupted through her as he laved and lapped apart ultrasensitive folds of flesh.

"Derek," she murmured, as the familiar tingling started in her tummy and spread outward until she knew it would be only moments before she came apart. Her fingers knotted in his hair as she tried to pull him away, wanting to prolong his delicious lovemaking, but he was relentless, his marauding mouth seeking her core. He licked and teased, lapped and tantalized until she crested, then she cried his name as her body started to convulse with the wave of pleasure pounding through her.

He didn't even give her time to catch her breath. He stood and grasped her bottom, lifting her off the ground. Instinctively, she wrapped her legs around his hips and eased down on his fullness, amazed at the sensations rippling through her with the first thrust of his hips. They instantly found their own special rhythm, and Derek encouraged her to come again, using his big body and erotic whispered promises.

She wanted to hold out, to make the wondrous sensations last forever, but he was merciless, driving into her until she thought she'd burst into a million pieces if she didn't come again. A cry tore from her chest and she arched against him at the same moment that he drove into her with one final thrust, her name falling from his lips on a strangled cry of pleasure.

The first thing she noticed as cognizance slowly returned was that the water had turned lukewarm. The second thing she noticed was the insistent ringing of the doorbell.

"Derek?"

His head rested against her shoulder, his breathing labored. "Hmm?"

She slid her hands over his back, reveling in the feel of solid muscle beneath her fingertips. "The doorbell's ringing."

He muttered a soft curse, settled her feet back on the porcelain surface of the tub, then kissed her hard on the lips. "Don't ya just hate those thirty-minute-or-less delivery policies?"

"I'd suggest we ignore it, but—" she smoothed her hand down his chest and reached for his warm and still semihard erection "—I have a feeling you're going to need to rebuild your strength...for later," she added with her most wicked grin.

11

TRACES OF pinkish light breached the sanctuary of the bedroom, along with the chatter of early-morning birds in the trees and Bronson's obnoxious snore sounding through the closed door. A cool, light breeze blew through the open windows, but before long, the heat of another summer day would be upon them.

Derek couldn't help but be a little resentful of that sunlight stealing into the room. In the light of day, the woman who was now curled against him in sleep would oppose him, lying between her pearly whites that she didn't love him. Last night, for those few hours of darkness, her guard had slipped, and he didn't need to hear the words he knew were in her heart. When they came together, it was in an explosion of heat and desire, of seeking and giving pleasure, and of love.

He stretched, feeling refreshed in spite of the few hours of sleep he'd managed during the night. Turning on his side, he crooked his elbow and propped his head in his hand, staring at her, memorizing every feature of the beautiful reason for his lack of sleep.

At the first stirring of arousal, a grin tugged his lips, his body confirming what his mind had already accepted: he simply couldn't get enough of

Doc Travers. Regardless of her staunch refusals to marry him, making love was one area where they were perfectly in sync. She drove him crazy and made him forget all about dumb rules and stupid charts and graphs and theories.

She stirred, turning onto her back and stretching both arms sensuously over her head. He took the advantage and leaned toward her, nuzzling her exposed neck, using his teeth and tongue to bring her fully awake.

She sighed and snuggled closer, wreathing her arms around his neck. "Good morning," she murmured, her voice a husky, sleep-filled whisper.

"Oh, it's gonna be," he promised, running a hand up the satiny leg draped over his hip.

He trailed little biting kisses down her throat and along her jaw while testing the weight of her breasts in his palms. They felt heavy and hot, and his own body's response was full and instant. He tugged the sheet down to her waist. Using his thumb, he teased her nipples until the dusky peaks hardened into tight buds begging to be tasted.

She sighed and closed her eyes again, her delicate hands traveling over the length of his back. With his teeth, he nipped at her still swollen lower lip, then soothed the spot with the tip of his tongue before taking her mouth in a deep, openmouthed kiss. He tasted her, loved her with his mouth, and felt the laziness of morning slip away as a sensual fire sparked, ignited and flamed.

Keeping their lips joined, he moved, pulling her beneath him. He settled between the natural, welcoming harbor of her thighs, the ridge of his arousal wedged intimately against her soft, moist curls. She rocked her hips and muttered something against his mouth he couldn't quite decipher. He'd figure it out later. He had a hot and willing woman making him crazy, and it was impossible for him to think of anything except pleasuring her.

Her soft gasp sent male pride surging through him when he left her sweet mouth to suckle her breast. He teased, he laved, shattering whatever defenses she might try to keep erected. He wanted her. He wanted her exposed, heart, body and soul, and his for the taking. He wanted to hold more than her breasts in his hands, he needed to hold her heart, because she sure as hell had his, whether she wanted it or not.

Sydney moaned softly when Derek shifted, the weight of his body sliding down the length of hers, his tongue creating a path of fire. She knew the scoundrel would take his sweet time about it, too, teasing her oh-so-close to the edge, only to hold the earth-shattering climax just out of her reach. During the long hours of the night, he'd kept her on the brink for so long she thought she'd go mad, until he finally brought her to a heart-stopping release only to fan the flames again and again until she thought she'd died and gone to heaven.

He ignited those embers now, fanning them with his tongue, stroking them with his hands and making her feel vulnerable and defenseless against the special brand of sexual power he had over her. She didn't protest when he used his fingers and his mouth in the most intimate way a man could pleasure a woman. She twisted her hands in the sheets as the tiny tremors shook her. He delayed her full release until she couldn't breathe, until she cried his name in a mind-blowing orgasm that shook her to the core.

Before she could gather her thoughts or calm her racing heart, he moved over her and pushed into her with one deep, hard thrust. She welcomed his body and the pure pleasure of their joining. She kissed him, tasting herself on his mouth, and clung to him, knowing that this time wouldn't be slow or gentle, but fast and hard, demanding and consuming.

She matched her movements to his, until he cupped her bottom in his hands, lifted her and buried himself to the hilt. Wild, desperate passion pulled at her, driving them both until reality shattered and only exquisite pleasure existed. She was burning up and half delirious as her body practically vibrated from the force of their lovemaking. Their bodies met and parted with increasing urgency while he ruthlessly held her where he wanted, driving deep inside her over and over again, each thrust pulling her closer, guiding her to the edge until she slipped over the side and cried his name yet again.

Afterward they lay together, chest to breasts, breathing hard as their hearts pounded in perfect rhythm. He buried his face in the crook of her neck and gently kissed her throat. Their bodies still intimately joined, he rose up on his elbows and looked at her, his eyes filled with a tenderness that made her heart ache. With equal tenderness, he gently brushed the moist tendrils of hair from her face and kissed her, long and slow. He kissed her the way he loved her, and dammit, she returned the kiss with equal emotion, refusing to say the word that would shatter the sweet bliss of their night together.

Goodbye.

She didn't know exactly when she'd come to the conclusion, but it had been sometime before she'd dozed off during the night. She felt like one of the creeps she'd dated on her search for paternity prospects, because she hadn't resisted his lovemaking. Instead, she'd greedily taken what she knew would never belong to her and had selfishly made love to Derek again.

She couldn't keep going on like this, seeing him every day, wanting him, but waiting for the resentment that would eventually settle over his heart. It'd be easier to deal with the pain now than later, once he'd become intricately woven into the fabric of her life.

He moved off her and rolled to his side, keeping her enclosed within the warmth of his embrace. She closed her eyes, breathing in his scent, treasuring the feel of his hands drawing lazy patterns over her back, and savored the moment for as long as she dared.

The cuckoo clock in the living room chirped the hour, and she knew the time had come to finally make him understand it wasn't fair to either of them to keep going on like this. Her heart did a little somersault beneath her breast at the idea of him no longer being a part of her life, but it was for the best.

Pain gripped her at the thought of life without him. Had she fallen in love with Derek? Was that why she was hurting and she hadn't even said goodbye yet? She'd made such a huge mistake in the past, but, she understood now, she hadn't really loved Nicholas, or at the very least, she didn't feel about him the way she felt about Derek. With Derek she felt complete, as if a part of her had been lost for years and she'd finally found what had been missing.

Oh God, she really *had* fallen in love with him!

"What are you frowning about?" he asked, pulling her tighter against him.

As much as she wanted to remain forever in his arms, she couldn't. She had to get out now and save them both.

You mean save yourself, her pesky conscience taunted.

Instead of answering him, or her conscience, she eased out of his embrace and left the warmth of the bed, and his body. She crossed the room and took the tattered blue terry cloth bathrobe from the hook on the back of the door. After they'd feasted on pizza, he'd thrown their wet clothes into the dryer, so at least she wouldn't have to wear his bathrobe home.

She tied the sash and turned to face him. He lifted up on his elbows and frowned at her. "Syd? What's going on?"

"Derek, we need to talk," she said. What she had to say was too important to be put off any longer.

He pushed a lock of dark hair away from his face, his frown deepening. "This sounds serious," he said, a note of caution in his voice. He swung his legs to the floor, but thankfully kept the sheet that was slung over his hips in place. She didn't know if she could go through with this as it was, and the last thing she needed was his nakedness distracting her.

She stuffed her trembling hands in the pockets of his robe and pulled in a deep breath, shoring up her courage. His hands were planted on his knees and he watched her, appearing nonchalant, but she knew enough about his body language to see the tension radiating through him. The intense look in his eyes told her he'd be ready to spring if necessary.

"I'm waiting," he said when she kept staring at him.

"We can't keep doing this," she finally said around the lump the size of the Space Needle clogging her throat.

He leaned forward and clasped his hands together between his knees. She resisted the urge to squirm under his direct gaze as he digested the information. "Somehow I don't think this is about your finally agreeing to marry me."

"No, Derek," she said, her voice catching. "I can't ever marry you."

"I see," he said calmly. Perhaps this wouldn't be as difficult as she'd imagined. "You never had any intention of marrying me, did you?"

Sydney couldn't quite believe what she was hearing. "I've been telling you all along I couldn't marry you." Why would he suddenly think she might have changed her mind?

His expression turned granite hard, emphasizing his determination. "You love me, Syd. What's the problem? What are you running away from this time?"

She felt his resentment like a sharp knife to her heart. "I'm not running away from anything," she said.

"That's bull," he said, and shot off the bed. He strode across the room to the dresser and yanked a pair of sweats from the drawer. He shrugged into them, then turned to glare at her. "You've been running ever since you came back from Kentucky."

"I explained what happened—"

"No," he snapped at her. "You told me what you wanted me to know. What else, Syd? What happened that has you too damned afraid to trust me?"

"I do trust you."

"The hell you do. What else did he do to you?" he demanded heatedly.

She'd been hurt when she first realized Nicholas had been using her. She understood now that it had been her ego more than her heart that had been wounded when she'd learned he was married, but that was nothing compared to the crushing pain in her chest caused by Derek's anger. Anger she knew stemmed from the hurt she was delivering him now. God, she knew making love to him had been a mistake, but why hadn't she realized exactly how complicated their lives would become? For someone who prided herself on depending on no one, she'd certainly made a mess of both of their lives.

She needed to move, to do something other

than stand in front of him with her emotions exposed and raw. "It's not that—"

"My love isn't good enough for you?" he demanded.

She knew it was the hurt making him lash out, but that didn't lessen the pain she was feeling. "It's not that. After we made love last night, I know this seems like—"

He muttered a gritty, heartfelt oath. "This isn't about sex, Sydney. It's about trust, and I want to know what you're so afraid of."

She wanted to turn away, away from the heat and anger of his voice, and away from the hurt in his eyes, but she felt rooted to the carpet. "It'll never work."

"Because you won't let it." He gestured angrily.

"I can't," she snapped.

His eyes glittered dangerously. "Why?" His suddenly calm voice belied his thunderous expression.

She turned away from him and moved to the window. She stared out at the backyard, at the edges of the green-and-white tablecloth fluttering in the morning breeze, and wrapped her arms around her middle in an effort to keep herself from falling apart. She'd do just about anything for him, but marrying him was asking for the impossible.

She let out a shaky breath. "For some reason I can't understand, you've gotten the crazy idea that you're the father of my baby. You might not be. There's a fifty-fifty chance that my child was fathered by artificial insemination."

"I keep telling you that it doesn't matter to me!" he roared, his frustration obvious. "Why can't you see that?"

"I can't, because it does matter!" she returned heatedly, spinning around to face him. "It might not matter to you now, but what about a year from now, or two years, or worse, ten years? What happens to us after you're completely ingrained in our lives? What happens when you start to resent the truth, that you're raising a kid who isn't even yours? What happens to the innocent child who adores you and calls you 'Daddy,' when you turn your back on him?"

He looked at her coolly, but she saw the deep pain flash in his eyes before he reined in the emotion. "I'd never do that, Syd," he said calmly.

She wanted to scream in frustration. He would, and she'd seen the pain and confusion in a little girl who didn't understand why the man she called Daddy treated her so coldly. There was no way she'd ever let her child suffer that same, heartbreaking fate. "You don't know that you won't," she cried. "And that's a risk I won't take."

He closed the distance between them and settled his hands on her shoulders. "You are wrong," he said gently. "You are so wrong. I love *you*, Syd. You're what matters to me. Your happiness and that of the baby you're carrying."

She closed her eyes briefly and struggled to keep the tears that were burning the backs of her eyes from falling. "It's not enough," she whispered.

The gentleness shifted, and hot, intense anger

filled his expression. "Why the hell not?" he demanded heatedly.

She shrugged out of his grasp. "Because I saw for myself what'll happen. When Nicholas's wife came to Kentucky, I saw how he treated his daughter. She adored him, but he kept pushing her away. And you know why? Because he *wasn't* the father. When he came to see me later that night to explain why he hadn't mentioned he was married, he told me. That's when I found out the truth."

"Oh, I'll just bet that was an honest declaration," he said, his voice laced with sarcasm.

"He told me that the little girl who followed him around all afternoon, hanging on his every word, practically begging for any scrap of attention he threw her way, wasn't his daughter. He said he knew Gwen wasn't his when he married his wife, but that even though it wasn't the girl's fault, he couldn't help the resentment. That sweet, innocent child suffered because he was 'stuck' raising another man's kid. I will not let you, or anyone, do that to my child."

He moved to the bed and sat on the edge. He braced his elbows on his knees and let his hands dangle between his spread knees. "Are you in love with me, Syd?" he asked her.

"What I feel for you isn't important!" she replied in frustration. "Didn't you hear what I just said? I'm not going to subject my child to what little Gwen suffered, because you'll end up resenting both of us in a few years."

"Answer me," he demanded in a dangerously

soft voice. He clasped his hands together and looked at her, waiting.

"Yes!" she said, unable to keep the accusation out of her voice. "Are you happy now? Yes, Derek. I do love you, and that's why I won't marry you."

His mouth twisted into a parody of a grin. "That's the most backhanded piece of logic I've ever heard, and believe me, I've put together some pretty weird logic the past month where you're concerned. You won't marry me because you *do* love me. Oh, that's rich, Syd. Care to explain this one to me?"

She turned away from that knowing grin and looked out the window again. A pair of chubby sparrows pecked at the grass, flying away once Bronson sauntered out the doggie door into the yard. The Dobie trotted beside the fence, sniffing the ground until he found his favorite shrub to leave his mark.

Finally, she turned back to face him. He sat there on the edge of the bed, looking at her as if he already knew the answer. "Because I couldn't stand it if you ended up hating me," she said honestly.

"And you're convinced I will if the baby isn't mine," he clarified. "Just like that son of a bitch who played you for a fool, right?"

She nodded and swiped at the tears clouding her vision.

"You need to trust me," he said in a quiet voice that held a wealth of warning that she may have just pushed him too far. He came off the bed and crossed the room to stand in front of her. She shifted her gaze from the firm wall of his bare chest to look into his eyes. He glared at her, and there was a shrewd, assessing glint in those sexier-than-sin eyes that increased her wariness.

She stuffed her trembling hands back in the pockets of his robe. "You're asking for blind faith. I can't do that."

"I'm not Adams," he said, in that same quiet voice she now recognized as cold fury.

The bands around her heart tightened. No, he wasn't Nicholas, but even that couldn't stop her from fearing that he'd end up hating and resenting her just as Nicholas had his wife and the child he'd signed on to love and protect. She wished otherwise, but the truth remained that she could not subject her child to that kind of pain. A parent was supposed to want the best for their child, and her leaving Derek now was the best thing she could do for her baby. Sadly, she shook her head. "It doesn't change anything, Derek. I'm sorry."

He gave her a hard-edged glare that ripped at her heart. Oh God, how she hurt. A crushing weight settled on her chest, and she ached physically. She'd known losing her best friend would be difficult, she just hadn't expected it to tear her apart like this. Better now than later, she reminded herself.

She walked away, opening the door and going down the hall to the laundry room for her clothes. The sooner she left, the better. Based on his growing anger, she knew they'd end up saying things they'd regret. And she had enough regrets to last her a lifetime.

She choked back a wave of tears and opened

the dryer, her determination to get through the next few minutes without crying faltering. She pulled their clothes from inside and folded his, then scooped hers into her arms. She turned, expecting to find him standing behind her with another series of arguments, but surprisingly, the hall was empty. Slipping into the bathroom, she dressed quickly.

Five minutes later, she stepped out of the bathroom to find Derek leaning against the wall, a heated expression flashing in his eyes that had nothing to do with passion, but everything to do with anger. His fury sliced through her.

Before she could guess his intent, he manacled her wrist and pulled her against him, then turned, backing her up against the wall until he surrounded her with his big, firm body. Her breath caught at the raw emotion and fury in his chilling glare.

She didn't want his anger, she didn't want this pain between them, but there was no going back. They'd crossed the line from friendship to lovers, and now it was over. There was no other way. It had to end.

But that didn't stop her from wanting his lips to claim hers in a kiss that would have her toes curling and her insides melting one last time. Nor did it stop her from wanting to slip her arms around his neck and press her body into his, and return that kiss with equal passion. Despite the coldness in his eyes, a sliver of hot need rose within her, sharpening the bittersweet ache in her soul.

"How dare you compare me to that low-life scum who cheated on his wife," he said, his voice tight. "Don't you know by now that I'd never hurt you?"

She blanched at his harshly spoken words. He was furious with her, and she didn't think he'd ever forgive her for letting her fear hurt them both like this. "I'm sorry," she whispered. "I never wanted this to happen."

He stepped away from her, as if he couldn't stand to be near her. "Make no mistake," he said, heatedly, "I'm not going to let any kid of mine grow up without a father. I lived it, Syd. I know what it's like."

"Derek. Please."

"Please what?" he returned angrily. "Let you off the hook? Let you keep hiding behind the excuse of unknown paternity? Not this time, Doc."

"But you—"

"Don't know if it's my kid." He finished the old argument for her. "Since you're so worried about the kid not being mine, then let's prove it once and for all." He closed the space between them, and the hard look in his eyes was unmistakable— he'd never forgive her for not trusting him.

And she couldn't really blame him.

"A blood test will erase the doubt," he said, the coldness in his voice matching that in his eyes. "And trust *this*, Doc. If it's my kid, you can bet it won't be the end of this."

He spun on his heel and strode down the hallway. He stopped at the bedroom door and gave her one last cold look, then stepped into the room and slammed the door closed.

The finality of the sound echoed through her, like a fatal blow to her heart.

12

SYDNEY DROPPED onto the sofa and punched the button below the red blinking light on the answering machine, then waited for the whirring of the tape to stop. A part of her hoped that Derek had called to tell her that he'd made a mistake and their friendship was worth salvaging, but she knew better. He'd made his feelings perfectly clear, and it had come down to his way, or no way at all.

She'd even expected him to forget about his silly demand that she go through with the blood test to determine the paternity of her baby, but unfortunately, he'd been adamant about that, too.

During the past three and a half weeks, the only time she'd spoken to him had been to return his call when he'd wanted the name of her gynecologist to make arrangements for the procedure. The test wasn't foolproof, but they would know with ninety percent certainty whether or not the baby was his. He'd been direct and to the point, and once he had the information he wanted, he'd abruptly ended the call.

What had hurt her the most was the lack of emotion in his voice. He'd sounded as if the past twenty-odd years of friendship hadn't even existed, but worse, as if the past two months that he'd been turning her world upside down had held about as much joy as a flea dip would for Bronson.

She felt miserable, and God help her, she missed him something awful. Garnering sympathy from Rachel had been useless. Once she'd confided in her assistant that she was pregnant, and that the baby could be Derek's, Rachel had read her the riot act. If she heard one more time that she was being unreasonable and selfish, she'd scream. And the last thing she wanted to hear again was how she was just being plain ol' stupid for letting a great guy like Derek slip away. When she'd tried to explain her position, Rachel had rolled her eyes and said she was her own worst enemy.

She had a nasty suspicion Rachel was absolutely right.

The tape stopped.

The machine clicked.

"The tests are back." Derek's deep voice resonated over the speaker.

The tiny thrill that raced through her at the sound of his voice crashed and burned at his brusque tone.

"We have an appointment tomorrow afternoon at one. See you there."

Tears blurred her vision, and she didn't even try to choke back the sob welling in her throat. She'd lost her best friend. The one person who'd always believed in her, who supported her, and dammit, who loved her even if she was being ridiculous or stubborn or unreasonable.

She didn't know if they could move past the

hurt. Taking their relationship back to the way it was before she'd made such stupid mistakes was impossible, but did that mean they couldn't heal and go forward?

Not unless you trust him.

Could she trust him? Could she put her faith in him not to turn his back on her and her child if he wasn't the father? Life was full of risks, and there were no guarantees, but she could do everything in her power to assure that her child would never suffer pain and rejection.

But what about denying her child the unconditional love of a parent? What would she be subjecting her child to if she denied Derek his rightful place in his son or daughter's life? Lord, she was so confused, she didn't know what was right any longer, except that with Derek she *felt* right.

Lifting her hand, she covered her eyes and let the sobs take over. This was why she didn't want to fall in love with him. Because it hurt so damned much.

She'd give anything to hear his husky laughter again, or hear the excitement in his voice as he told her about research far beyond her realm of comprehension. She even considered selling her soul to see that wicked twinkle in his eyes when he looked at her.

She sniffed at the silliness of such an idea. "Ridiculous," she muttered, wiping the tears from her face with the back of her hand. "You don't have a soul left to sell."

Because it already belonged to Derek.

THE WAY Derek figured it, he had one shot left. He was in an all-or-nothing situation, he thought as he punched the button for the tenth floor. And he wasn't about to leave his future to chance, or to the whims of a woman too stubborn to see the truth. Even if the truth landed in her living room via an asteroid with a huge neon banner proclaiming they were meant to spend the rest of their lives together, she still wouldn't believe it.

The elevator halted at the tenth floor, and he waited impatiently for the silver doors to slide open, then strode down the designer-decorated corridor to the walnut double doors at the far end leading to Dr. Hutchinson's office. He took a deep breath, mentally rehearsing his speech one last time, then pushed open the door.

He'd intentionally arrived thirty minutes early because he hoped to have a serious man-to-man with the guy who held his future in a manila folder. The waiting room was deserted except for a young woman who didn't look any older than nineteen, gently rocking a baby carriage. He nodded to her, then approached the receptionist's window.

A middle-aged woman he didn't recognize from his visit three weeks ago looked up at him and smiled. "Can I help you?"

"I'm here to see the doctor," he said.

The receptionist gave him an odd look. "Sir, you must want Dr. Rosen, the urologist, at the other end of the hall. We get a lot of his patients in here by mistake. This is a gynecologist's office," she added in a stage whisper.

The young woman behind him snickered, then coughed to hide her amusement.

If his and Sydney's future hadn't been on the line, he just might have found the situation slightly amusing himself. "No, I'm here to see Dr. Hutchinson."

Her salt-and-pepper brows pulled together in a frown. "Are you sure? He doesn't see men as a rule."

"I'm sure," he said.

She gave him a skeptical look. He didn't want to know what she was thinking.

"Derek Buchanan. Why don't you check the schedule?" he suggested, trying not to sound too patronizing.

She shrugged, then ran her finger over the names neatly typed on the list in front of her. Her brows shot up when she stopped at "Drs. Buchanan/Travers, 1:00 p.m."

"My mistake, Dr. Buchanan. Dr. Hutchinson is with a patient, but he'll be with you shortly."

Derek nodded and turned from the window. The young woman rocking the sleeping baby smiled up at him, then bent her head to fuss over the infant. He peered into the carriage at the tiny little body sleeping soundly beneath a pink cotton blanket, and smiled.

"How old is she?" he asked, amazed at the perfection of the little girl's fingers curled beside downy sable curls. Would his son or daughter have Sydney's wild sable curls, or his straight black hair? Would he or she have Syd's luminous green eyes, or blue?

"She's six weeks today," the young mother said with more than a touch of pride in her voice.

She gently adjusted the blanket around her daughter, then settled back in the mauve chair.

Derek moved closer to the carriage and leaned over, breathing in the fresh, powdery baby scent. "She's awfully small."

"Most babies are," the mother answered, a note of humor in her voice.

"Dr. Buchanan?" the woman behind the reception desk called. "Dr. Hutchinson said you may wait in his office if you'd like until Dr. Travers arrives."

He straightened and nodded to the receptionist. "She's beautiful," he said to the mother, then followed the receptionist to Hutchinson's private office.

He waited until he was alone, then sat in one of the leather chairs opposite the desk. That lasted for all of three seconds, and he shot out of the chair and started pacing. He needed to talk to Hutchinson before Sydney arrived. He checked his watch. Twenty minutes to one, so he still had time to convince Dr. Hutchinson to perform a breach of ethics that would assure him a future with Sydney.

SYDNEY STEPPED off the elevator ten minutes before the scheduled appointment. As she'd showered and dressed for the meeting that would alter the course of her life, she'd given serious consideration to telling Stewart Hutchinson she didn't care about the results, but she knew she'd be lying to herself, and to Derek.

Or would she?

She was so confused, she didn't know what to

think any longer. The only thing perfectly clear in her mind was that she had to somehow mend the ever widening gap between her and Derek.

She slowly walked down the corridor toward her doctor's office, wondering what would happen to them if the test proved Derek was the father of her baby. Had she caused so much damage to their already precarious relationship that they'd be reduced to awkward silences during scheduled weekend visits? Or could they at least resume their friendship for the sake of their child?

But what if it's not his baby? she wondered, and stopped cold. The sudden realization that she wanted this baby to be Derek's crashed over her. If the test proved with ninety percent certainty that he wasn't the father, she might never see him again.

She bit back a sob as tears threatened to spill again. That was something she could not allow to happen.

As difficult as it was to admit, she did love him. Just the thought of her life without him left her feeling empty. She didn't need a man in her life, but she needed Derek with a certainty that surprised her. He was her mate. Her true soul mate.

And she knew he loved her. For the past two months he'd done everything in his power to show her how much he cared about her, from his insulting but endearing practical reasons they should marry, to his misguided attempts to show her how much richer her life would be with a husband around to share all the little things on a day-to-day basis.

He was so ingrained in her life, she couldn't

imagine being without him. And if the past weeks weren't enough to convince her how empty her life would be without him, then nothing would. She knew exactly where she wanted him—in her life, and her baby's.

Their baby!

She hurried to the end of the corridor, hoping to find him in the waiting room so she could tell him she didn't need a test to prove anything to her.

All she needed was him.

She stopped at the door and gathered her courage. Considering the weak footing she'd been on lately, and one mistake after another she'd made with him, not to mention the constant rejections, she prayed he hadn't given up on her. With one last deep breath, she opened the door and stepped into the crowded waiting room.

She gave her name to the receptionist, and was surprised when she was sent right to Stewart's private office. As she neared the door marked Private, she heard the sound of male voices. The quiet and calm one she recognized as her gynecologist's. The other louder one was distinctly Derek's.

Curious, she inched closer to the door, which was open a mere crack, but enough for her to hear their conversation clearly.

"What you're asking isn't merely a breach of ethics, Dr. Buchanan, but also a breach of my patient's trust."

"I don't give a damn about your ethics," Derek practically shouted. "A child's future is at stake."

"The child's future, or yours?" Stewart asked

calmly, using the soothing tone Sydney had always found oddly comforting whenever she had to bear the indignity of one of *those* exams.

Derek's reply was ripe, and she cringed. "What difference does it make?" he replied. "All I'm asking is that you tell her I'm the father. Why is that such a crime?"

Stewart sighed, and Sydney couldn't help wondering if that never-ending patience he always exuded was being stretched to the breaking point. "As I explained, implying anything other than what the test results indicate would not only be a breach of professional ethics, but a breach of trust. My patients expect a certain amount of that trust, and I refuse to lower my standard, even for something as important as this appears to be to you. I understand—"

"No, you don't understand!"

Sydney inched closer and peered through the door. Derek paced in front of the doctor's desk. His hair was mussed, as if he'd been running his hands through it, and his eyes blazed with a combination of anger and frustration. God, he looked as if he were fighting for his life. And in a sense he was—for their life together.

"Look, Doctor," he said, coming to a halt in front of the desk. "She's one hell of a stubborn woman. She loves me, but unless she's absolutely certain this kid is mine, she's going to keep refusing to marry me. I've told her it doesn't matter if the kid's mine or not, but she won't listen to reason."

She waited, and after what felt like a lifetime,

Stewart asked, "You're sure it's going to be enough for you?"

"I love her. That's enough for me."

"Derek," she said, and pushed opened the door. "Don't."

He didn't even look at her, but stood with his hands on his hips, dropped his head and shook it in what she assumed was defeat.

"Derek, it's enough for me, too."

He slowly lifted his head to look at her, but she ignored him and gave Stewart her attention, so she wouldn't lose her courage. "I thought knowing without a doubt that Derek was the father was the most important aspect of assuring my child's happiness, but I was wrong. What's important is a father who will love him unconditionally."

"Syd—"

She lifted her hand to stop Derek before he could go any further. She kept her gaze riveted on her doctor, afraid if she looked at Derek she'd throw herself in his arms and beg him to forgive her for being so stupid.

"You see, Stewart, Derek's right. I was being stubborn." Her voice caught and she sucked in a shaky breath. "Stubborn, and selfish, and determined to do it all on my own. I thought I could give my baby everything he needed. I could love him, care for him, provide for him, and ensure that he had the best that I knew how to give him. But I made one drastic error in judgment."

She turned her attention to Derek, no longer caring that she was crying. Taking the two steps necessary to close the distance between them, she lifted her hand and gently cupped his warm cheek in her palm. "What I can never give him is his father's love. Only you can do that for him."

The love shining in his deep blue eyes touched the part of her she'd so foolishly and selfishly tried to keep to herself—her heart.

"Her," he said, then reached for her and pulled her into his arms to hold her tight. Which was just fine with her, because she had no intention of ever letting him slip away from her again. "We could have a her."

The clearing of a masculine throat drew her attention. "Stewart, I'm sorry to put you through all this trouble. But could you please destroy the results to that test?"

Derek looked down at her, his brows pulling together in a frown. "Syd, are you sure? I know how important this is to you. If you really want to know, I'll understand."

She looked up at the man she loved with all her heart and soul. She still harbored fears, but with time and Derek's never-ending patience, she knew they'd eventually dissipate and fade into the background. Her past had brought her to this point in her life, and as painful as it had been for a time, she wouldn't change a moment of it.

"It's just some dumb test that has a ten-percent margin of error, anyway. It's not important, Derek. You're what's important to me," she said, using the words she'd fought for too long.

"No sense getting all upset over something that's not even positive," Stewart said, tucking the file under his arm. He rounded the desk and headed toward the door. "I've got patients waiting. Sydney, I'll see you in two weeks," he added firmly.

He stopped with his hand on the door and looked back at them. "Would you be interested in knowing the sex?"

Sydney looked at Derek. "I don't think so."

Derek quirked a dark brow. "It might be helpful if we knew," he suggested. "You know, so we can decorate the nursery, and decide what kind of clothes and toys we need to buy."

Stewart shook his head in disbelief. He'd seen some strange things during his years of practicing medicine, but today's events topped the list.

"You'd better start working on names now," he said with a grin, pulling open the door. "Because in about seven months the two of you are going to have to come to some kind of an agreement."

He stepped into the corridor and closed the door behind him, giving his patient and her—he shrugged—husband-to-be, a few moments alone.

"Here," he said, handing the chart to his nurse. "Why don't you pull the test results and seal them in an envelope so they aren't inadvertently given to the patient."

The nurse took the file and opened it. "I don't understand," she said, frowning in obvious confusion. "Don't they want the confirmation of Dr. Buchanan's paternity?"

Stewart grinned at his nurse. "They didn't need the results to tell them what they both already knew."

Epilogue

Four years later...

SYDNEY REACHED into the back seat of her new minivan and flipped the latch holding her son in the car seat. "Oh David, what have you done now?" she asked the three-year-old when he held up the truck she'd just bought him. Or rather, what was left of the new toy.

She took the toy from him and dropped it into the diaper bag, then lifted the boy out of the van. "Sweetie, Mommy doesn't buy you new toys so you can break them."

"Not boken, Mommy," he said, his blue eyes serious. "I fix it."

"Okay, you fixed it," she said, and ruffled his dark curls. It really wasn't fair, she thought, turning her attention to the sleeping Danielle. Her son had had thick, luscious curls almost from the day he was born, and her poor daughter had only a slight dusting of color on her crown.

She turned at David's squeal of delight, and smiled when she saw Derek hefting the boy into the air, then tucking him under his arm like a football.

"David destroyed another toy," she said, slinging the diaper bag over her shoulder, then gently lifting Danielle and her portable car seat into her arms. "It only took him ten minutes this time."

"I'll fix it," Derek said, setting the boy on the porch, then crossing the yard toward her.

She lifted a brow at him. They'd come to the conclusion long before David was born—if she couldn't repair whatever needed attention around the house, they'd hire a professional. Lord knew it saved them tons of money in the long run, because Derek still couldn't tell a Phillips from a flat-head screwdriver, no matter how many times she showed him the difference.

"Okay, you fix it," he said with a sheepish grin, taking their sleeping daughter from her and planting a quick kiss on Sydney's lips.

Her life had certainly changed in the past four years, she thought as she went about her evening routine. By the time they managed to get their active son down for the night without too much argument, and Danielle bathed, fed and into her crib, she was ready for some long-awaited quiet time with her husband.

She found him on the patio, peering into the telescope he'd set up to teach David the stars and planets, a subject in which her son had already started showing signs of interest. "I still think they're prettier just looking up at the sky," she said, coming up behind Derek and slipping her arms around his middle. "You lose the magic by looking through that thing."

He straightened and moved her around in front of him so her backside was pressed against his firm thighs. With his arms around her, he bent and nuzzled the side of her neck. "The only magic

I'm interested in is the kind you hold over me." The husky rumble of his voice skirted along her nerve endings and settled low in her tummy.

She sighed and stepped away from him, trailing her hand along the back of the porch swing. "Speaking of magic," she said. "I saw Stewart today."

That got his attention just as she hoped it would, considering today had been her six-week checkup after giving birth to Danielle.

"And?" he prompted with a hopeful note in his voice that made her smile.

He turned and looked at her. Tingles of awareness shot through her when his eyes darkened with a passion that hadn't ebbed even after four years of marriage. And regardless of her gynecologist's warning to be careful for thirty days until the birth control pills he'd prescribed had time to take effect, she had a serious case of lust for her husband that was close to getting out of control.

He stepped away from the telescope and slowly walked toward her, his intent and purpose evident. Anticipation thrummed through her, and her heart rate picked up speed.

"Answer me, Syd. What did he say?" His voice was deep and husky, and completely intoxicating. He stopped inches away. All she had to do was reach out, slip her arms around his neck and pull him close to find herself in heaven.

He leaned forward, his eyes darkening, causing the blood to race through her veins. Her fingers itched to touch him, to trace the outline of those corded muscles, to run her hands over the hard wall of his chest and feel his heartbeat beneath her palm.

"That we can make love," she finally whispered. Fire licked through her at the first brush of his lips. Before she had time to draw her next breath, he pressed his body into hers and captured her lips in a mind-blowing kiss.

He slipped his hands down to her bottom and urged them closer together, man against woman, sex against sex. She whimpered and moved her hips against him and felt his control slipping. She couldn't believe she'd once equated loving Derek with emotional suicide. *Talk about foolish mistakes,* she thought.

He lifted his head and looked down at her, all the love in her heart evident in her gaze. She smiled up at him, knowing she'd made the right choice in trusting him. Because he'd given her more than love in return, more than two beautiful children as an expression of their love.

In return, he'd given her his heart, and the promise of heaven for the rest of her life.

If you enjoyed what you just read,
then we've got an offer you can't resist!

Take 2 bestselling love stories FREE!

Plus get a FREE surprise gift!

"Don't miss this, it's a keeper!"
—**Muriel Jensen**

"Entertaining, exciting and
utterly enticing!"
—**Susan Mallery**

"Engaging, sexy...a fun-filled romp."
—**Vicki Lewis Thompson**

See what all your favorite authors
are talking about.

Coming October 1999 to a retail store near you.

 **HARLEQUIN®**
Makes any time special™

WIN A DREAM

In celebration of Harlequin®'s golden anniversary

Enter to win a *dream!* You could win:

- A luxurious trip for two to
  The Renaissance Cottonwoods Resort
  in Scottsdale, Arizona, or

- A bouquet of flowers once a week for a year
  from FTD, or

- A $500 shopping spree, or

- A fabulous bath & body gift basket, including
  K-tel's *Candlelight and Romance* 5-CD set.

Look for **WIN A DREAM** flash on
specially marked Harlequin® titles by
Penny Jordan, Dallas Schulze,
Anne Stuart and Kristine Rolofson
in October 1999*.

FTD

ℜ
**RENAISSANCE.
COTTONWOODS RESORT**
SCOTTSDALE, ARIZONA

K-TEL